THAT GOOD HEX

M.J. CAAN

VINCI

BOOKS

By M.J. Caan

Singing Falls Witches

Vinci Books

vinci-books.com

Published by Vinci Books Ltd in 2025

1

Copyright © M.J. Caan 2020

A CIP catalogue record for this book is available from the British Library.
Paperback ISBN: 9781036705589
The EU GPSR authorised representative is Logos Europe, 9 rue Nicolas
Poussion, 17000 La Rochelle, France contact@logoseurope.eu

Chapter One

Torie Elizabeth Bliss was far too angry to sleep. She lay in her bed, staring daggers at the ceiling.

Literally.

She used her magic to summon knives from the kitchen, flinging them upwards to become embedded in the timber crossbeams that adorned the vaulted ceiling in her mother's bedroom. No, scratch that. She had to stop thinking of it as her mother's home. This was her house now. At least her name was on the deed, so that made it hers.

Her mother was still here, just in a non-corporeal form.

"A ghost," she said, speaking aloud to herself. "Mom's a ghost, and now I've inherited her house. And her powers."

With a sigh, she sat up, swinging her legs over the side of the bed. She had to sit there for a moment, stretching her back and letting a brief wave of dizziness pass before she could stand.

Getting old sucked. Well, getting older sucked. She wasn't old yet.

With a thought, she sent the knives flying back into the

kitchen to the butcher block in which they rested. She was getting better at manipulating physical objects with her mind; a trick that had taken her longer to master than she liked.

She made her way to the kitchen and took a cup and a box of tea selections from one of the cabinets. Double green matcha sounded nice. Placing a bag into the cup, she settled at the large island while she waited for the water to come to a boil.

The thought of using magic to heat the water briefly flashed through her mind. She dismissed it just as quickly. She had discovered she wasn't so good with generating fire. It was easy enough to call on, but controlling it was still a little outside of her grasp, as she had quickly learned when she tried to light the fireplace without the aid of a match.

That was a lesson the singed white mantle wouldn't let her forget any time soon.

She watched the kettle and removed it from the stove at the first sign of a whistle. Her mind was swimming, and she hoped the soothing, hot liquid would lull her enough to fall asleep.

Try as she might, she couldn't quiet her thoughts. Nor could she stop them from zeroing in on her ex-husband, Ward. She hated that he was clawing away at her conscience this way. She had finally managed to put him and his deception behind her. But, like chronic back pain, he showed up in her life again.

Well, not him, per se, but the woman he had left her for.

Torie's mind flashed back to the encounter in the bakery with the beautiful fae who had approached her and her friends with a request.

Word had spread around town that they had been behind solving Singing Falls' supernatural serial killer.

When the town's police department had failed them, two witches and a shifter had stepped up and stopped the killer.

Well, they had help from a werewolf, but Jasmin had said that wasn't something that should be spread around. Not just yet at least. The town was made up of peaceful shifters and gentle paranormal creatures. Most of them feared the more predatory paranormals from the supernatural world.

And werewolves sat at the top of the nightmare ladder for most of the town's paranormals.

But the fact remained that Torie and her friends had reached minor celebrity status among the townsfolk and, before long, they had started approaching Torie and asking for help.

Simple things for the most part; performing magical background checks for businesses hiring new workers, infidelity investigations, and lots of removal of curses from family heirlooms. Who knew that hexed jewelry was such a big thing in the community?

But the minute the fae flowed into the bakery where Torie sat with her friends—Jasmin, Fionna and Elric—she sensed something was deeply disturbing the fae. She hadn't mastered the art of reading auras, but she knew anguish when she saw it.

That anguish was transferred to Torie when the woman told her why she needed their help. Her daughter had disappeared, and the fae needed them to help find her. Of course, the fact that her daughter was the woman Torie's husband had left her for only complicated the matter a teensy bit.

Torie sipped her tea as she remembered the look of pain in the fae's eyes.

"She's my only child," the fae had said. "I don't know what I would do if something happens to her."

Despite wanting to throw the picture of Wednesday, the fae's child and her husband's mistress, Torie thought about her own son, Shawn. What would she do if he suddenly dropped off the face of the earth and she couldn't reach him? She'd move heaven and earth to find him, that's what she would do. Why would it be any different for this fae?

The two of them might come from different worlds, literally, but that didn't mean they weren't tied by the bond of motherhood. Torie had asked the woman to sit down and tell them everything.

Afterwards, she had exchanged numbers with the fae and told her she would reach out to her the next day in order to start a formal investigation into her daughter's disappearance.

Her friends had been quiet after that. The jovial atmosphere had died down, and Torie had decided it was probably best if she went home. She had promised to call them the next day to discuss finding the missing person. One who had run off with her husband. She had mentioned who the woman was, but she wasn't ready to go into any details with her friends just yet.

She made her way back to her mother's house and crawled into bed, clothes and all, pulling the covers up around her head.

That was hours ago. Now she sat in the kitchen, the soft pendant lights illuminating the space with an antique glow.

"Why so solemn, daughter?" Her mother appeared beside her in a shimmer of light.

Torie jumped so hard tea splashed across the island.

"Jesus, Mom, don't do that!"

She wasn't sure she would ever get used to her mother's ghost just materializing unannounced like that.

"I swear, if it wouldn't just pass right through you, I'd hang a bell around your neck," she said.

Her mother smiled. "Well, you were the one who called to me."

Torie furrowed her brow. "No I didn't." Had she? Granted, she had been thinking more and more about the fae and her daughter, which made her think about being a mother, which inevitably led her to think about her relationship with her own mother. "And even if I were thinking about you, that doesn't mean I need you to pop in like that."

She tried to sound gruff, but the truth was, she was very happy to see her mother. She wanted nothing more than to throw her arms around her; but that wasn't quite possible.

"So, what's wrong?" her mother said.

Torie sighed. "We were at the bakery and this lady—a fae—showed up and asked for our help."

"But isn't that what you do now? Help the people of the community?"

"Well, yes, but this was a different kind of request. She needs help finding her daughter."

Alva Bliss placed a transparent hand over her mouth. "That poor woman. Of course you will help her. What is the problem?"

"I wouldn't so much call it a problem as a complication. Her daughter is the woman Ward left me for."

"No! If I could fall out on the floor right now, that's what I'd do. Are you sure?"

Torie nodded. "Very. I spent a few years getting to know that woman. Well, as much as I could, I guess. I know it's her. No doubt at all."

Her mother was silent for a moment before she spoke up. "So, what are you going to do? Do the girls know?"

Torie sipped her tea before turning to her mother. "They know who she is. I couldn't hide my reaction. But I didn't tell them any details; not there in front of this grieving fae. I just didn't have the heart. I mean, of course I'll help...but..."

"But it could mean confronting Ward about what he did. For all you know, he's not even in the country anymore."

"Chances are he isn't. I mean, if the FBI can't find him, then what chance do I have?"

Her mother clicked her tongue at her. "Are you serious? The FBI doesn't have magic at their disposal. You're a witch. Your bastard ex-husband can't hide from your hexes."

Why hadn't she thought of that? Was it possible to track down a missing person with magic?

But didn't Jasmin warn her about using magic for her own personal gain? She mentioned as much to her mother to see what she thought.

"Well, Jasmin is right. To use magic for your own gain would invite trouble. However, in a case like this, you wouldn't be doing it for you. It would be for that poor fae woman who needs to know her child is safe."

Torie hadn't thought about it like that. She wanted to help, and this seemed like an easy way to accomplish a task.

"Thank you, Mom. I'll think about that."

And by think about it, she meant she would run it by Jasmin and Fionna first thing in the morning.

"So. Care to tell me what is really bothering you about all of this?" asked her mother.

"What do you mean?" Torie could feel herself avoiding the question. It was a bad habit she had…playing dumb or repeating a question that made her uncomfortable to buy herself time.

"Don't play games with me, Torie. You've always done that; even as a child. And I hate it just as much now as I did then."

Torie let out a long sigh. "It's Ward, Mom. I just don't know if I want to confront him. I mean, finding Wednesday means finding him as well. Things are going so good here. I'm in a great place in my life…I never realized how miserable I was in my old life. I guess seeing him just means facing the old Torie again. I'm just not ready to do that."

Her mother smiled her ghostly grin. "But, darling, don't you see? It's not the old you that you need to face; it's Ward and his view of you. You were always more than what he saw you as. You're starting to realize that and you're afraid you'll have to prove it to him. But what you're not realizing is that you don't have to prove a damn thing to anyone. You have become who you were always meant to be. He just didn't see it."

And with that mic drop, the ghost was gone. Dissolving back into whatever ether she resided within when she wasn't visiting with her only child.

Torie finished her tea and then moved into the living room where she collapsed onto the large, comfortable couch, pulling the plaid quilt over her head until she drifted off into dreamless sleep.

The next morning, she awoke with renewed energy and focus. She thought about her conversation with her mother and realized that the specter of Alva was right on so many levels.

Torie had spent so many restless nights thinking about what Ward had thought of her. Where she had gone wrong with him. What could she have done better? What would it have taken to make him stay?

So many self-doubts had crept into her consciousness.

But not once had she thought about what he should have been doing. Marriage was a two-way street. Why did it always fall to the woman to do the right thing in order to make sure that a relationship worked?

It took two to tango, and she realized that during their dance, he had been stepping all over her toes for years.

She closed her eyes and offered a quick prayer to the High Mother for seeing fit to let her see another day on this earth. In her old life, she had never been a spiritual person; but now, having come into her power, she understood that there were so many forces of nature at work around her. She also knew that she needed to give thanks to those forces. In the grand scheme of things, she was a small, insignificant gnat.

Each day she was allowed to walk this earth, she would honor the spirits and the powers that be, by being the best person she could be.

And that meant letting go of her old life with a man who betrayed her, and embracing a new life as a witch with the power to hex.

She made her way to the kitchen, threw on the kettle and rummaged through the refrigerator for some eggs, herbs and cheese. She knew Jasmin and Fionna were on their way to see her, and she would greet them with fresh morning tea and omelets.

Then, she was going to tell her friends everything, and they were going to figure out a spell that would let her find her bastard husband and the child of a grieving fae.

Chapter Two

When Jasmin and Fionna walked into the house that morning, they were greeted with the smell of strong coffee, eggs, bacon, biscuits and an array of jams and jellies.

"Wow," said Fionna, "what's the occasion? And how early did you wake up to get all of this ready?"

"I was up early," Torie replied. "So, I decided to whip up a little something for my closest friends."

"Um, are you expecting more friends to come by, because, girl, you got enough food here to feed the needy," said Jasmin.

Torie laughed. "Not at all. I was feeling restless and once I got started, I just didn't stop. Grab a plate and help yourself."

The food was laid out on the large kitchen island and the women took up stations around it.

"Oh my, this is so good," said Fionna, biting into a biscuit with butter and raspberry preserves loaded on top.

"So," said Jasmin, helping herself to the steaming coffee, "I know this is deeply personal for you, but do you want to talk about what happened yesterday and what you're feeling now?"

"Yes," said Torie, her voice low as she picked at the bacon on her plate. "I'm sorry about the way I just kind of faded out on you all, by the way. You know I want to help her, right?"

"Of course," replied Fionna. "We all do. But this is something you get to make the call on."

Torie took a deep breath. There was really no other way than to just rip the band aid off and dive right in.

"That daughter of that fae, Wednesday? She was not only Ward's business partner, but I considered her a friend of sorts as well. I let her into my life. Might as well handed over the keys to the marriage bed to her as well."

Silence filled the space. Fionna stopped mid-chew to stare at her friend, and Jasmin sat perfectly still, the mug of coffee halfway to her lips.

Slowly, she placed the coffee cup down. "Are you freaking kidding me? What kind of woman has so little respect for the bonds of friendship?"

"I wish I were kidding," said Torie. "But yeah; that's her."

Fionna finished the bite of biscuit before clearing her throat. "So, what do we do?"

"What do you mean?" said Jasmin. "That's easy. The fae is on her own of course."

Torie looked at her in surprise. "No. Absolutely not. She came to us for help finding her child. We need to help her."

Jasmin narrowed her eyes. "Or we tell her that her daughter isn't missing; that she is on the run from the authorities because she's involved in a scheme to defraud people. And that she's doing it with a married man, no less."

"You heard what that woman said," Torie replied. "She said the bond she shared with her daughter wasn't there anymore; that it was like the woman

had just disappeared. What if something happened to her?"

"And?" said Jasmin. "You mean, what if something happened to your ex by extension."

Torie didn't reply, reaching for her own coffee to sip instead.

"Well, so what if that's what she meant?" said Fionna. "She's had no closure from all of this. Maybe we kill two birds with one stone. We help find the girl, and if that allows Torie to confront her ex and get that closure, then so be it."

Jasmin regarded both of us closely.

"And what about Elric?" she asked. "How does he fit into all of this?"

Torie felt heat rising into her cheeks. The truth was, that was part of what was racing through her mind.

"I mean, aren't you two an item?" asked Jasmin.

"I...I don't know what we are," Torie said. "He has been instrumental in helping me settle in here, just like the two of you. And we certainly wouldn't have stopped that hedge witch without his help."

"So does that mean you think we should ask his help with this too?" asked Jasmin. "How do you think he'll feel about helping us track down a missing person that could lead to you finding your ex-husband?"

"Okay, first, can we stop saying ex-husband? Technically, we are still married. And that's part of why it's important that I find him. I want to properly end this marriage so I truly *can* move on."

Both Jasmin and Fionna were quiet at that.

It was something Torie had often reminded herself. Their lawyer had told her that in time the courts would dissolve their marriage if she filed for it, but without Ward, it could take years. Especially with the mess he had left her in as far as the fallout from his crooked business dealings. If he were to reappear and be taken into custody, that would certainly streamline the process for her; helping to create a clean break from him.

Was she ready to see that? To see Ward hauled off in shackles? How would that affect Shawn? He was so angry at his father; would it help or hurt matters for him to have closure as well?

"I just need to move on," said Torie. "Ward made his decisions. I'm in a different place in my life right now and I don't want to take any steps backwards."

Jasmin nodded. "I understand. But I also know the pull the wrong man can have on you. Especially one that was part of your life for such a long time."

There was a faraway look in her eyes that filled Torie's mind with questions. But she knew enough about her friend to understand that when Jasmin was ready to talk, she would.

"So, all that being said, that's why I asked you both over here." Torie stood, taking her coffee cup to drop in the sink before turning back to her friends. "I was thinking about how we go about finding a missing person. Especially one that is on the run and even the authorities can't track down. My mother had a good idea; is there a magical way to do it?"

"Oh...that sounds fun," said Fionna, clapping her hands together.

Jasmin frowned, deep in thought. "That could be tricky. Harder than you might think."

"What about a tracking spell?" Torie asked. "Like the one you tried with that serial killer? That worked."

"That was because we had a sample of the killer's blood to power the spell. Do you have some of Ward's blood handy?"

"Gross," said Torie. "I most certainly do not."

"Do you have anything personal of his? Something that ideally would have been a part of him? Hair perhaps?"

Torie thought back to what she had brought with her from New York. Had she perhaps picked up a comb of his and thrown it in her overnight bag when she left the mansion?

"I'll have to check," she replied. "But I literally moved here with just the clothes on my back. And by now, I seriously doubt there is any way to get back into the house. All our property has been seized by the government."

"Oh! What about Shawn?" said Fionna. "They share the same blood. Would that work?"

"Absolutely not!" said Torie. "I mean, even if it was possible, I would never involve Shawn in any of this."

"Agreed," said Jasmin.

"There have to be other options," Torie said. "What about a locater spell to tell us where he is? The tracking spell is to take us to him; if that's too complicated, then how about one to just pinpoint him on a map?"

Jasmin rubbed her chin, deep in thought. "I don't know. If it were just him, then maybe. But the fact he is in the presence of a fae could block the spell. Fae are notorious for their ability to be invisible to spells. Honestly, if they do not want to be found, then they can't be found."

"You know, speaking of that, how did he meet a fae in the first place?" said Fionna. "Even here in Singing Falls, it's not like they are hanging out on every street corner. Most of them live in the forest, only coming into town on a few occasions."

"I think that's something we ask her mother," said Jasmin. "Assuming we are all in agreement that we want to take this on. And any fallout that may come from it."

Fionna and Torie nodded.

"And Elric and Max?" said Jasmin. "I think we should at least keep Max apprised of what we are doing. As the town sheriff, he has a right to know if we are trying to track down a member of the community who might also be involved in federal crimes."

"There's no might to it," Torie said. "She and my husband swindled millions from innocent people."

"Okay, so that's a yes on Max. But maybe we don't bring Elric into this unless we have to."

Torie shook her head. "No. I may not know what is going on between us, but if he and I are to have any shot at something resembling a relationship, I'm not keeping anything from him. I'll tell him tonight. After we get back."

"Oh, where are we going?" asked Fionna.

"To that fae's house. If we're going to track her daughter down, maybe she left clues as to where she and Ward were planning to run to." Torie stood to clear the dishes.

"We'll get those," said Jasmin. "You cooked; we clean. Plus, you have the fae woman's number. Give her a call and let her know we'd like to stop by to ask a few questions."

"Oh, this is so exciting," said Fionna. "We are like a real team now. Hey, what should we call ourselves? Oh! What should we charge?"

Both Torie and Jasmin stopped what they were doing.

"Charge?" said Torie. "I guess I never considered that. I

mean, why would we charge to help people? Plus, it's not like any of us need the money."

"True," said Jasmin. "But we don't have to charge a monetary fee."

"What then?" asked Fionna.

"Well, the fae are famous for their spirit gems that they collect. Those are very rare magical items. We could ask for a couple of those as payment. And if we decide to make this a full-time occupation, then we collect magical fees from our clients based on who and what they are."

Torie ran this through her mind. She had no idea what a spirit gem was, but it sounded intriguing.

"I guess that would be okay, as long as it didn't create a hardship for the person we're collecting from," she said. "And, of course, I don't want to say no to someone that needs us and has nothing to offer in exchange."

"I like that," said Fionna. "We'll be like *Law and Order* but without having to go around in long coats all the time. Or having to be mean to perps."

"Wouldn't go that far," chimed in Jasmin. "Never know when you might have to crack some eggs to make an omelet."

Torie went to her room to retrieve the card with the fae mother's name on it, when Fionna grabbed her by the elbow.

"I just had a thought. What if all of this does bring Ward back into your life, and instead of closure, you both realize what you mean to each other." Fionna's eyes grew larger as the story she was weaving in her mind grew. "But then, you realize what Elric means to you, so you are torn and have to decide between your two great loves! You could be like Bella in *Twilight*! It would be a love triangle for the ages."

Both Torie and Jasmin looked at her like she had just grown a second head.

"Girl, what have you been munching on before you came over here?" asked Jasmin. "Cos whatever it is, you need to be sharing it."

Torie laughed at the thought. "Fionna, I can promise you there is no…what did you call it—a threesome—going on here."

"I said a love triangle," said Fionna. "Two *very* different things."

"Well, whatever it is, I can tell you there will be no tri-anything happening. Who has the time and energy for all that? I have better things to do with my day than sit around pining after two different men. Ward made his bed. He can roll around in it all he wants to for now, because I promise you I will not be joining him."

"Amen, my sister," said Jasmin. "Ain't nobody got time for that silliness."

"Bella did," huffed Fionna.

"And how did that work out for her?" asked Jasmin. "Knocked up by one, and the other one falling in love with her baby. That's some nonsense written by someone who has probably never been involved with a real man." They all laughed at that. "I mean, in real life, she should have left both them crazy, jealous fools alone and got with that sweet guy she went to school with."

Torie couldn't help but laugh, grateful for her friends who were taking her mind off her estranged husband and his shenanigans.

She looked at the card, and then took her phone out of her jeans and flicked at a few numbers before placing it to her ear.

"Hello, ma'am…this is Torie Bliss. We spoke yesterday

at the bakery." She waited, nodding and smiling to herself. "Yes, that's right. I hope I didn't catch you at a bad time. But I wanted to let you know that my friends and I would very much like to help you with finding your daughter. As a matter of fact, we'd like to come over and discuss things in person. We have some questions we'd like to ask." Again, she nodded, listening to the person on the other end of the line.

"That would be great. And..." she stopped speaking, frowning. When she resumed talking, her voice was lower, a slight tremble to it. "No, I can assure you that will not be a problem. Okay, that's fine. We will see you in a couple of hours."

She hung up the call, returning her phone to her pocket as she turned to face her friends.

"Everything okay there?" asked Jasmin.

Torie nodded. "Fine. She just said that a stranger had been by her house. Asking about her daughter and if she knew where she was."

"If she was involved with Ward, and the feds are tracking him, stands to reason they would be interviewing Wednesday's family as well," said Jasmin.

"Perhaps," said Torie. "But she said the man who came to visit her said he was a witch. And that he would be happy to track her daughter down for her."

Chapter Three

They all piled into Jasmin's Subaru and pulled out of the drive, following the robotic turn-by-turn directions emanating from her navigation system.

"I thought only women were witches," Fionna said once they were underway.

"What about warlocks?" Torie said. "I mean that's what I grew up learning a male witch was called. Samantha's father on *Bewitched* was a warlock."

Jasmin glanced disapprovingly at her out the corner of her eye before turning her attention back to the road.

"What did I tell you about equating the supernatural with things you've seen on TV or the movies? However, in this case…I have never known there to be male witches. We gain our powers from mother earth, and that is a connection men cannot know."

"Why?" asked Fionna.

"Because men cannot have babies for one thing, and that, the ability to create life, is literally a force of nature. Also, men's bodies don't go through the changes ours do as we age. While I'm not entirely sure, I believe that is another reason we get our powers later in life as well."

"Well at least nature is on our side," said Torie.

"What do you mean?" said Fionna.

"She means that for the most part, the world revolves around men," answered Jasmin.

"Exactly. If you ask society, men are praised as they get older," said Torie. "Silver hair on a man, desirable. Silver on a woman, haggard. We get older and are blessed with spreading hips and waistlines and told to stop wearing skirts and buy only cover-ups for swimwear. What do men get? Dad bods."

"What's a dad bod?" Fionna asked.

"A free pass to keep eating ice cream after every dinner. And not just any old ice cream; no, not the fat-free yogurt, but full-fat Rocky Road with whipped topping and sprinkles. That's what a dad bod is. Oh, and apparently it makes all the neighborhood babysitters go into heat at the site of them."

"Sounds like someone just got their nerves touched," said Jasmin, smiling.

"I'm sorry," said Torie, "it's just not fair. They get lauded for being more attractive as they age, and we get…to become invisible."

"Well, not in this town," said Jasmin. "Here, women are every bit the equal of any male—supernatural being or not. Also, the majority of the paranormals living in Singing Falls come from a society where the females are often the alphas. But even so, no one is held in any higher regard than anyone else based solely on their sex. So you won't find any of that dad bod shit here."

"So what you said about the changes we go through as

we get older, do you think that somehow preps us for our powers?" Torie asked.

"I do. As we age, we become more open. Our senses often become sharper...hence the change in the taste of food some older women experience. I also think we begin to experience the touch of magic, even when we don't realize it. When I was going through the change, there were times when I thought I wanted to climb out of my skin because it was so...I don't know; itchy. That was the beginning of my being able to sense the ley lines around town."

"Ley lines?" asked Torie.

"Mystical lines that connect points of power around the world. They form a grid that the earth's natural power runs along. They are particularly strong in this area. You'll develop a sense for them as you get more acquainted with the town."

"Can only witches feel them? Can you sense them, Fionna?"

The squirrel shifter smiled and nodded. "I can. Most shifters can feel them in our animal forms. But, unlike witches, we can't interact with them."

"So, basically, what you're saying is that getting older isn't a curse for us," Torie said.

"Not at all. I would consider it a blessing."

"But wouldn't you trade places with a twenty-year-old Chosen One," asked Fionna, playfully. "You know, if you could be Buffy for a day, would you?"

"Hell no." Jasmin laughed. "That girl was always getting distracted by vampire dick. She had one job...save the world, and she couldn't decide which vampire dick she wanted first. All that strength wasted on a child."

"Okay, but you have to admit, Spike was a hottie," said Fionna.

Jasmin laughed. "I mean, I wouldn't kick him out of bed for eating crackers in it...but I'd save the world first."

"Sometimes I miss the body I used to have," said Torie. "When I was younger, I played a lot of tennis. Kept me in great shape. Now, I get winded walking up a big hill. In a town filled with supernaturals, I should be in better shape."

Jasmin huffed. "Please. That's part of the joy of being older. No rules of engagement. Them young ones might have strength and flexibility on their side, but I'll take age and treachery any day of the week."

Fionna and Torie howled with laughter, only to be interrupted by the robot Subaru voice telling them to turn right and their destination would be on the right.

The only problem was, there was no road to turn right on.

Jasmin eased the car off the road as the three of them glanced out the passenger side of the car at a meadow that led to a line of trees obscuring any further view.

"What now?" questioned Fionna.

"We walk. Like I said, most fae live off the grid. They have homes deeper into the woods, where they feel more secure. I'm betting it's right through those trees."

They got out of the car and crossed the sun-kissed meadow. Grass and reeds were almost knee deep in places, but the entire field smelled of flowers and wet moss; spicy and sweet at the same time.

As they approached the tree line, Torie could feel herself tensing up. She still wasn't fond of the woods, and Singing Falls seemed to have been carved out of an old growth forest. Everywhere she went in the town, they were never far from sprawling acreages of old growth.

"It's okay," said Fionna. "I don't smell anything. These woods are safe."

"Agreed," echoed Jasmin. "I'm not sensing anything. Are you?"

Torie stood still, letting her senses expand. She had no idea how to "feel" for something, but she had to admit that nothing felt off to her. She shook her head, and the three of them ventured into the stand of trees.

It wasn't long before the canopy of leaves knitted together enough to choke off the sunlight, creating a beautiful shadow world of deep reds, greens and browns.

"Why is it always so quiet in the woods?" Torie asked.

"It's not quiet," said Fionna. "You're just used to the sounds of civilization. If you know what to listen for, the forest is bustling." She stopped and cocked her head to one side, pointing to her left. "There's a stream about a half mile to our left. Deer are drinking at it as we speak. There are beavers chewing wood to build a damn a little farther downstream. Ahead of us, there are two large owls forming a hunting party; I can hear the smaller critters skittering away from them, cos they know hungry predators when they see them. To our right, there's a small cave, or something hollowed out of the ground. Sounds like something big is sleeping in there...so I think it's probably best that we keep away from that."

"Wait, you can *hear* all of that?" queried Jasmin. "Cos I'm with Torie, I don't hear a thing."

"Shifter ears," Fionna said. "I grew up in the woods. Trust me, you're never alone once you enter them."

"Okay, Ms. Grizzly Adams...so which way to the fae's house?" replied Jasmin.

Fionna turned her head slowly before pointing to a barely perceptible path to their left.

"This way. I can smell freshly cut wood, and smoke from a fire."

They let her lead the way, choosing to walk in silence as both Torie and Jasmin strained to hear a fraction of what Fionna had picked up.

Finally, Torie couldn't take the silence any longer.

"So, what made you want to leave all of this for life in town?" she asked. "I can see how at home you feel here."

Fionna smiled. "When I was a child, I could not have imagined ever leaving the small meadow I grew up in. It was like paradise to me, with what seemed like limitless land to explore. Now, mind you, in my squirrel form, an acre of land might as well be the Amazon. But as I grew, my surroundings began to shrink. It's hard to describe. I found myself wandering farther and farther away from our home.

"My parents didn't try to stop me; they knew I needed to find my place in the world. One day, I ventured into the outskirts of Singing Falls and found a whole new world to explore. The sounds and scents drove me wild. I had to understand this magical place. It didn't take me long to recognize other shifters. They were everywhere...or at least it seemed that way. Then I met Taylor." She hesitated, swallowing hard at the memory of her late best friend. "We became instant besties. We would explore the woods around Singing Falls, getting to know all the paranormals who lived here. I knew, this was where I belonged. The humans scared me at first. Until then, I had somehow gone my whole life without interacting with one. The only ones I knew were the occasional hunter that would venture into my woods. I'd sit in the tops of the trees, very still, watching them.

"They terrified me, with their loudness and their guns... for so long that was all I thought humans were. But then I met this little witch here, and pretty soon the three of us became inseparable."

"Yeah," huffed Jasmin, "until you ran into a new nurse

graduate that stumbled into the bakery one morning. You lost your heart that day, and we lost our third wheel."

"Hey, what can I say? The heart wants what the heart wants."

"You two make a great couple," said Torie. "So, can I ask? Did Glen have a hard time with your…secret?"

"Well, she was a little freaked out at first. Okay, she was a *lot* freaked out. But once she realized I was who I was because of *what* I was…she came around. Now, look; she doesn't bat an eye at witches, werewolves or even vampires…though she says she never wants to meet a vampire if she doesn't have to; not that I blame her."

Her eyes hardened, and Torie knew she was thinking about Arnold. Fionna was a forgiving soul, yet Torie wondered if she would be able to forgive the vampire that had killed her best friend. He had also killed Torie's mother, and part of her had wanted him dead when they had fought. But there had already been so much death in the tiny community, Torie couldn't imagine willfully adding to the body count.

"You know, at some point, we'll have to be around Arnold again," Jasmin said softly. "He's dating Eddie now, and Eddie is still our friend."

Fionna's head snapped around to stare at her.

"Yes, and let's not forget that if Arnold had his way, Eddie would be dead as well. What is he thinking, getting involved with that monster?"

"He realizes that Arnold wasn't in control of himself when he did those things. We need to give him some grace," said Torie.

"Grace?" screeched Fionna as her eyes began to sting with bottled-up tears. "Arnold killed my best friend. He killed your mother. He killed shifters in our community. And for what? Yet, you would excuse his behavior?" Anger made her voice tremble.

"Not excuse him but realize that he was being controlled by something else. Something that we still haven't found," added Jasmin.

She is right, thought Torie. Singing Falls might have regained its peace and tranquility on the outside; but inside, there was still something that stalked them all. Something that was behind the hedge witch who had controlled Arnold and made the vampire do all those horrible deeds.

Fionna grew quiet, brushing away her tears as they continued through the woods.

Torie sought to break the uncomfortable silence. "So, Jasmin, what about you? What drew you here to Singing Falls?"

"Oh, that's not really important right now," she said sheepishly.

"Oh, she came here for a man," said Fionna. "Isn't that right, Jasmin?"

"Whatever my reasons, now is not the time," replied Jasmin. She lifted her hand and pointed. "We're here."

Ahead was a house unlike any Torie had ever seen. It was carved into an embankment, nearly disappearing into the forest. A thatched roof jutted out from the hillside, with two glass windows that peered out from underneath like watchful eyes. Large Juniper trees flanked it on both sides, further adding camouflage to the home. A single red door stood out from the overgrown hillside in which the house rested. From the top of the hill there was a single gray chimney jutting skyward, from which smoke trailed upward into the forest canopy.

"Told you," said Jasmin, "the fae prefer to live in the woods."

"It's beautiful," Torie breathed. "I've never seen anything like it."

As they stepped up to the door, Torie grasped the large brass knocker and lightly banged. They stepped back and waited, looking at one another.

"Maybe we should have brought a breakfast cake," said Fionna. "It's rude to show up empty-handed like this."

"Somehow I don't think she will mind," said Jasmin.

When no one answered, Torie knocked again.

"Hello," she called out, listening for any signs of movement.

"Maybe she stepped out," suggested Fionna.

Torie frowned. "She knew we were coming. That doesn't seem likely."

She reached for the door handle, and it turned without the resistance of a lock. She looked at Jasmin who just shrugged her shoulders. Torie pushed the door inward and slowly took a step inside.

The inside of the house was not what she had expected. The outside might have looked like something from *Lord of The Rings*, but the inside was traditionally furnished with teak and leather, and comfortable cloth wingback chairs that flanked an ornate wood burning fireplace.

The three of them walked in, Torie again calling out to announce their presence. The living room led into the kitchen, and as they stepped inside, they stopped as one, instinctively clutching one another.

There, in front of the large, double range, was the fae. She was face down on the floor, her skin a pale, lifeless gray.

Chapter Four

The three deputies were going over the house, dusting for fingerprints and checking the door for signs of forced entry.

Torie could feel the butterflies in her stomach churning as she went back over her statement with Max. The wolf stood with pen and pad in one hand as he read back what she had told him.

"So you didn't see anyone else? No sign someone had been here?" he asked.

Torie shook her head. "No. We arrived and knocked, like I said. The door was unlocked, and we came in...and found her just like that."

"And you just walked in because you were expected?"

"That's right. We had spoken earlier on the phone and she knew we were coming over."

Max scribbled a few more notes just as one of his deputies approached.

"No sign of forced entry, Sheriff. So far, we haven't found any prints either. Well, only the ones on the door handle." The deputy gave Torie a side-eyed glance.

Max nodded. "Torie, we're going to have to have you come to the station to be printed." He held up a hand before she could protest. "It's just to compare to the ones on the door handle so we can exclude you from the suspect list." He leaned in close, his voice dropping to a whisper. "So, did you pick up anything mystical in nature off the body?"

Torie's body stiffened. "What? No. Why would you ask that?"

"Oh yeah, I forgot you're still new at this. Did Jasmin get any readings? I only ask because I didn't catch any scents at all in the house; only the fae and yours."

"I have no idea what Jasmin may or may not have picked up. You'll have to ask her."

Fionna approached and leaned in. "I didn't smell anything either. It's weird, there is no death scent at all."

Torie shifted her weight uncomfortably from one foot to the other, throwing her arms around herself. "What do you mean by that?"

"When something dies, it has a certain smell as it begins to break down. The smell is immediate and can linger in the air for a very long time. But in this case," said Max, "There is nothing."

"Exactly," said Fionna, "I can see the body there, but if I close my eyes?"

"It's almost like it disappears," finished Max.

Fionna nodded. "I've never been around a dead fae; maybe that's how they pass. But I doubt it."

Jasmin approached the three of them and joined in. "Max, I don't suppose we could have a few minutes alone in the house once everyone clears out, could we?"

The sheriff regarded them and then nodded.

"I think I can arrange that. But only if you keep me in

the loop with whatever you find." He started to walk off but then turned to Torie. "How's Elric?"

His voice was short and clipped, but somewhere in the bass of the tone, Torie could hear the caring in his timbre.

"He's good. Great actually." She paused, trying to read the older werewolf. "You know, you can come by for a visit if you'd like. He's setting up an apartment of his own...I'm sure he'd welcome seeing you."

Max arched an eyebrow, and Torie could swear she saw his lips draw back in a slight snarl.

"Nah, that's okay. I'm sure I'll run into him at some point. Okay. As soon as the coroner hauls the body out, and the deputies clear out, you can have the place to yourselves."

"Thank you, Max," said Jasmin, watching as the sheriff moved away, barking more orders at his men.

"What was that about? Asking about Elric but then acting like he couldn't care less?" said Torie.

Jasmin shrugged. "He's probably still smarting that Elric opted not to join his little deputy squad. It's gotta hurt to have a beta around for years, and then suddenly have him just break away."

"That's so sad," said Fionna. "But why can't he just say that?"

"Men," said Jasmin. "God forbid they admit to having feelings or caring about one another. The two of them would rather sulk around and waste energy trying not to run into one another than admit they miss each other."

Torie nodded. Even big, bad wolves could have hurt feelings it seemed.

"So, what are we going to look for inside the house?" she asked.

"Not sure," said Jasmin. "But something about this doesn't sit right. No way is this a natural death."

"You don't think she could have just…I don't know… collapsed?" asked Fionna. "Maybe she despaired over her missing daughter."

Torie shook her head. "No. It would have been the opposite. A missing child would have given a mother the strength to withstand anything until she knew her baby was safe."

"I agree," said Jasmin. "Plus, when we walked into the house, there was nothing present. Usually when you enter the abode of a magical being, you can feel it. But this time, it was like everything had been sanitized."

"I know what you mean," said Fionna. "And you're right, Torie, I may not be a parent, but I know how I'd feel if something ever happened to Glen. I'd hang in there till the bitter end."

They waited, milling around the front lawn of the house and watched as the fae's body was removed. They had zipped her into a black body bag and placed her on a stretcher. It would take all the deputies and the coroner to get her from the house out to the main road. There was no way to get a vehicle through the woods.

A thought flashed through Torie's mind as she watched them struggle to push the stretcher towards the tree line.

"Hey, where is her car? How did she get into town?" Torie asked.

"Fae, like many of the supernaturals that remain in the forested areas, don't drive," said Jasmin. "They have ways of getting around. Some even have magical portals that take them from place to place. They don't have need of anything as mundane as a car."

"But if she didn't die a natural death," continued Torie, "then whoever may have been involved most likely would not have been able to get in and out of here the way she did, right?"

Jasmin nodded slowly. "Of course. If someone else was here, they might have been able to scrub the house clean, but..."

"They might have left a clue somewhere back near the main road," said Fionna. "I'm on it."

With that, she shifted into her squirrel form and sprinted back the way they came.

"If there is any kind of clue out there, she'll find it," said Jasmin. "Now, you and I will examine the house through a magical lens."

Jasmin pushed open the door, but this time, neither of them entered. Instead, Jasmin closed her eyes and reached out with her magic, feeling for anything that didn't feel like it belonged.

Torie watched, once again cursing the fact she was such a newbie.

"I don't feel anything unusual as far as the threshold goes. If someone else was here, they didn't force their way inside."

Torie felt a chill creep up her spine. She couldn't imagine anything worse than being attacked in your own home by someone you trusted. She tried not to think about her mother at that moment.

Or the vampire responsible for her death that Torie had opted not to kill.

They walked in slowly and began to go over everything in the living room intently. The deputies had been thorough in their search, but they lacked the one thing Torie and Jasmin had on their side.

Magic.

Jasmin reached into her large purse and withdrew a round crystal lens that was attached to what looked like a set of brass knuckles. She slipped her fingers through the rings so that the crystal stood up above her hand. She then raised her arm, hand pointed outward, so the lens was at eye level. Then she began sweeping the room slowly, peering through the crystal intently.

"What is that?" asked Torie.

"Scrying crystal," replied Jasmin. "It lets me detect magical signatures that are trying to hide."

"Is it picking up anything?"

"Not yet. But I'll comb every inch of this house; maybe I'll get a hit on something."

Torie stepped away, letting her work. She looked around, noting all the dusting powder the deputies had left everywhere. She made her way through the back of the house to the comfortable bedroom. There was yellow police tape across the door frame, blocking off the room. She hesitated for a second, then decided to duck under the tape and enter the room.

It was simply appointed; a single rocking chair, dresser and a large, four-poster bed. The drawers were all open. The deputies had been thorough in their search.

Torie racked her brain, trying to remember every cop and investigation show she had ever seen. What would they do next? There was always a clue to be found, you just had to know where to look.

Unless of course there was no crime committed.

Could it be possible that the fae truly had killed herself? Or just passed away? Do supernatural creatures have heart disease that they could succumb to?

No. That just didn't feel right. She thought for a

moment about next steps. She might not have a scrying crystal, but she did have an idea. She stood in the center of the room and closed her eyes, then whispered a spell into being.

"I call on powers, from eons gone by,
show me what remains, hidden from my eye."

She felt a tingle behind her eyelids that turned into a tickling that spread across her face as her magic snaked outward in response to the invocation.

Opening her eyes, she saw the room bathed in an eerie blue glow. Everything directly in front of her stood out crystal clear, but the periphery of her vision was darker and out of focus. She stumbled as she began to walk around; magical tunnel vision was a bitch.

Still, as she walked around the house, she could see the light of her vision change from blue to hazel, to varying shades of dark green depending on what she looked at. She entered the kitchen. The gait of her walk and the fact she was holding both arms in front of her like a zombie caught Jasmin's attention.

"Torie? What are you doing?"

"I…I'm not sure," she replied.

Once in the kitchen, she looked around and noticed the light around one of the cupboards turned a color she had not seen before. The cabinet glowed a deep orange, with the center of it turning an alarming red.

"There's something in that cabinet," Torie said, pointing to the one in question.

Jasmin opened it to reveal a stack of porcelain plates on one shelf and some smaller, cake plates on the shelf above them.

"I don't see anything," she said. "Wait, let me try with this…" she held up the scrying glass and peered through. "Well, what do you know?"

She placed the crystal lens back in her purse and lifted up the plates, removing one that looked identical to the rest. It was bone white, with a solid silver rim. To Torie's enhanced vision, it glowed red hot.

"What is that?" she asked.

"It sure isn't a plate," said Jasmin, setting it on a small table in the corner of the kitchen.

She held her hands over it, eyes closed.

"It's fae magic. A particular kind of glimmer spell they use to make one thing look like it's something else."

"Can you break the spell?" Torie asked.

"Don't have to. When the person that casts a spell like this passes on, the spell dissipates as well. This one will fade in time, but I think we can give it a little boost."

She leaned over the plate and whispered kindly. "You've done your job. Whatever secret you were keeping for your mistress is no longer needed. She has moved on to a better plane. You don't have to remain hidden. I promise you, we are friends, and you don't have to be afraid."

The plate shimmered on the table, turning smoky as it slowly dissolved from view, leaving only a single silver key with a half-moon on one end with a small silver chain attached to it.

"Wow," said Torie, "you didn't even have to use magic for that."

"The fae are very spiritual. They often invoke forest spirits to invoke their magic. This little guy just needed to know that he could return to the woods now."

"One more thing for me to learn I guess," said Torie.

"Don't be hard on yourself. A few months ago, you

didn't even know this world existed. It will take you some time to learn paranormal lore. But hey, you were the one who found this. Nice spell you conjured."

Torie smiled, trying not to blush. She was too old to be moved by another's compliments, and yet, it was something she also needed to hear.

"So now we have a key," Jasmin said, "what do we do with it?"

Torie's eyes lit up and she snapped a finger. She dug around in her purse and withdrew the picture the fae had given her on the day they met in the bakery. Jasmin stood next to her as they peered at the photograph of Wednesday together.

There, barely visible against the woman's white blouse, was a pendant. It was a perfect match for the silver key the two witches held.

"Well," said Torie. "Looks like we need to find whatever this key unlocks, and it will at least bring us that much closer to finding Wednesday, and maybe figuring out who, or what, killed this fae."

"Well, I know what this key unlocks. It's for a safe deposit box in a vault that caters to the supernatural."

There was a skittering sound coming from the room behind them and they turned in time to see Fionna scamper into the kitchen and shift back into human form.

"Fionna," said Jasmin, "what did you find?"

"You were right. There was another car parked not far from where we were. There was a male scent that I couldn't quite place, but I tracked it through the woods and then it disappeared in the clearing just across the glen from this house."

"A male witch," said Torie.

"So it would seem," added Jasmin.

"We found a key that was hidden away with magic. Hopefully it will open something useful at this secret vault Jasmin knows about," said Torie.

Jasmin cleared her throat. "There's just one thing. The vault is in the basement of Arnold's law office. If we want to get into it, we need to go visit the vampire first."

Chapter Five

That evening, Torie focused on cooking dinner for herself and Elric. He had spent the last couple of days painting his apartment. Once she returned from the fae's house, Torie realized it was time for her to tell him everything that had happened since they were at the bakery. He sensed something; of that she was sure, and she knew how she used to feel when Ward kept things from her.

She doubted Elric would drive himself crazy with nonsense scenarios the way she used to, but she wasn't going to risk it. They had a good thing going, and while she didn't know where things with the werewolf were going, she wanted them to have a decent and honest shot at whatever life might be handing them.

She decided on a meal of ground-lamb burgers, grilled onions, homemade tzatziki, and a watermelon and feta salad. She had almost forgotten how much she loved to rattle the pots and pans. By the time she heard his knock on the front door, the house smelled of fresh chopped herbs, ground coriander, and lamb.

"What is that smell?" asked Elric as he walked through the living room towards the kitchen.

"Is it that bad?" Torie asked coyly.

"Only if you consider divine to be a bad smell, cos whatever it is, it smells like heaven."

He leaned over and gave her a quick kiss. He had one hand behind his back and whipped it in front of him with great theatrical relish. A beautiful bouquet of calla-lilies greeted Torie, tickling her nose with their sweet fragrance.

"Elric," she said, "They're beautiful!"

He didn't reply but went about finding a vase big enough from the workroom just outside the kitchen. Once it was filled with water, he placed them on the large kitchen island, away from the space where Torie was chopping. They warmed the space and brightened it just the right amount.

"So," he said, "what can I do?"

Torie hesitated. In her marriage, she had never been offered help in the kitchen. Ward's idea of providing help was to say, "I really wish you'd let the help do that." That had always given Torie pause. She never knew if he said that because he thought what she was doing, fixing dinner for her husband and their child, was beneath her; or was because her cooking wasn't really that good and that was his way of passive-aggressively telling her to leave it to the professionals. Either way, it had given her a complex about being in the kitchen.

One that she had just started to get over.

But Elric was different. She was starting to learn that there was nothing duplicitous about his words. If he offered it, then he meant it. So she decided to take him up on it.

"Well, first, can you go light the grill? And then, cut up the cucumber, and mince some garlic?"

"With pleasure." Elric left the kitchen, and Torie listened as he made his way through the workroom and out onto the back patio.

She smiled. Was he whistling as he fired up the grill? He seemed truly happy and at ease, and that made her happy. She hoped he would keep that mood after their talk.

He came back in, washed his hands, and took up station beside her as he started to peel the cucumber.

Torie walked to the refrigerator and took out two prepared red drinks, setting one down in front of him.

"What are these delicious-looking creations?" Elric asked.

"Watermelon martinis. My own special recipe."

He took a sip, made an appreciative puckering sound with his mouth, and arched his eyebrows. "Wow. Strong and tasty. Well done. So, how was your day?"

Torie took a deep breath. "Interesting that you ask. I was hoping to talk to you about some things."

She took a sip of her drink and cleared her throat. She returned to the refrigerator and took out a packet of ground lamb meat and added it to a glass mixing bowl.

"Do you remember that fae who approached us in the bakery? The one who asked for help finding her daughter?"

Elric nodded. "Do you want these sliced?"

"Um, quarter the slices please. I need chunks, but not too small. So anyway, this fae. As it turns out, her daughter is the same woman that my... that Ward, left me for."

She didn't look over at Elric but sensed a slight hesitation in the sound of his knife making contact with the cutting board before he resumed his chopping pace.

"If we help her, it may mean that I'll run into Ward again at some point."

"Are you worried about that?" asked Elric.

"No, I'm not. I mean, I'm not worried for me. But I wasn't sure how you would feel about it."

He stopped chopping and looked over at her. "Me? You don't need to consider my feelings in this."

She turned to him. "Of course I do! I mean, I don't know where we are headed with things, but I do know I like you. I respect you, and I would never do anything to hurt you."

He smiled. "This will not hurt me. This woman...this fae, I can imagine she is in a lot of pain; not knowing where her daughter is. She has come to you for help. Who could say no in such a situation?"

Torie felt her eyes water as she returned to the bowl of meat in front of her. She dumped in some coriander and began measuring some ricotta in as well.

"Well, speaking of the fae; me and the girls went over to her house today to ask some follow up questions about her daughter."

She added an egg, a few more spices, and began mixing it all together by hand.

"And?" pushed Elric.

"She was dead. We found her dead in her kitchen."

Elric stopped what he was doing and turned towards her, his face a mask of concern.

"Are you okay? What happened?"

"I'm fine. A bit shook up from it, but there was nothing we could do."

"Why didn't you call me? I would have gone with you."

"Honestly, it never occurred to me. I thought this would be a quick question and answer session with her."

"Do you know how she died?"

"No. The coroner took her body, so I'm assuming they'll do an autopsy. We checked the house over, physically and magically, and all we found was a key that matches one that Wednesday, her daughter, was wearing in a picture we have." She paused, gazing down into the bowl before continuing nonchalantly. "Oh, one other thing, have you ever heard of a male witch?"

Elric went tense. "Yes, why do you ask?"

"When I spoke to her on the phone this morning, she said that she had been approached by a male witch who had offered to help her find her daughter. Jasmin has never heard of a male witch. She didn't think they existed."

She sensed the tension in Elric's body as he went back to slowly chopping the vegetables.

"Elric, what is it?"

He sighed deeply. "I think you need to let this go. If the fae is dead, then there is no need to continue looking for her daughter."

Torie stopped what she was doing, walked over to the sink and washed the raw meat off her hands before she moved over to Elric and placed a hand on his.

"Talk to me," she said.

"Jasmin is correct, in a way. There are no male witches, at least they are not found in nature. But there are men who are born with certain sensitivities to wield the mystic arts. While they can manipulate magic, they can't generate it themselves. They need to steal their power from a source."

Torie felt a cold wetness start to form along her spine. "What is the source they use?"

"Another magical entity; typically, a female witch. They enslave the witches and use them like batteries, drawing the power out of the women for their own perverse desires. And when they have drained the witch to the point she is no longer of use to them, they kill them."

Torie felt a shiver and the hair on the back of her neck stood up.

"Torie, if there is a male witch in this town, then he is here for a reason. And it isn't to help a fae woman find her lost child. You, Jasmin, and every other witch in this community is in a lot of danger."

Torie's mind was spinning. She needed to tell Jasmin about this immediately.

"That's why I want you to drop all of this. I'll find Max and we can scout for this male witch. But until then, I think you and Jasmin should leave town."

Whatever fear she was feeling vanished in a haze of red at his words.

"I most certainly will not. I feel like I've only just stopped hiding away from the world. I'm not going to fade away again because of some...man witch. I mean, we took down a vampire...I think we can handle someone that has no powers of their own."

"Torie, male witches collect female witches, use them up, and cast them aside. They have developed powers that allow them to do that. It's what they have evolved to do. I don't even know all they are capable of, and I don't relish the thought of crossing paths with one. I certainly don't want you in one's cross-hairs."

"You know an awful lot about the dark side of supernaturals," Torie said.

"Yes. I have seen some shit. Maybe you'll remember that the next time you decide to go off into the woods chasing a fae."

Torie gave him a wry smile and took her phone out.

"I'm calling Jasmin. She needs to know about this."

She swiped at the screen a couple of times and raised it to her ear.

"Jasmin, you need to get over here quick. Elric just gave me some info that you really need to hear... What? No, you don't need to pick up Fionna. I think she said it was date night with Glen. I'll tell you as soon as you're here. Okay. See you then."

She turned to Elric, suddenly realizing what she had just done.

"Elric...I'm sorry. I just realized that we were having date night as well. You know I didn't mean to imply that Fionna's relationship is more important...I just..."

"It's alright," he said, playfully. "I didn't think anything like that. Your friends are important to you, so their safety is important to me as well."

She blushed, resting her head on his shoulder and giving his strong arm a squeeze.

"Hey, what about dead witches?" she said, her head snapping up off him. "Do I need to worry about my mother? Can he hurt her spirit?"

Elric's brow wrinkled as he thought about her question. "You know, I have no idea. Up until recently I had never had an encounter with a ghost like your mother. I have no idea what can and cannot harm her."

Torie thought about it and decided that she would call to her once Jasmin arrived. If there was a threat to witches in town, then she needed to know about it as well. Even if she was incorporeal.

"You know, it might be smart for all of us to sit down one day and let you school us on all the things that go bump in the night that aren't too friendly," she said, sipping on her drink once again.

"Yes. Don't think that every paranormal creature is as friendly and cuddly as the ones here in Singing Falls. You'd be surprised at the kinds of monsters that are out there."

Torie smiled. Despite the fact there was some kind of witch-draining, male leech out there, she felt safe with Elric around.

The doorbell rang before she could let him know just how thankful she was to have him around. Setting down her drink, she headed for the door.

"Well that was quick, Jasmin. How badly did you break the speed limit?" She swung the door open and suddenly felt like she had been punched in the stomach.

"Hello, Torie. Don't suppose we can come in, could we?"

Ward stood on the other side of the door, his black duffel bag slung across one shoulder. He stepped aside, revealing Wednesday standing behind him. As shocked as Torie was to see them, she was even more shocked when she looked down Wednesday's body to the very large baby bump she was sporting.

Chapter Six

Torie was aware of the fact she was standing there with her mouth literally hanging open, her eyes comically large and unblinking.

"Ward? What...what are you doing here?"

"I—we—need a place to lay low for a minute, just till we can regroup. Wednesday's mother lives here in town. We were going to her place, but Wednesday can't reach her by cell, and she said that never happens. We thought maybe the FBI had somehow gotten to her and were watching the house. But I remembered that your mother also had a place here, and I was pretty sure the feds hadn't made the connection as to who she was, so we were hoping...anyway, when I saw your car in the drive, I figured it wouldn't hurt to ask."

Torie was dumbfounded. She was too much in shock to be angry.

"But how did you know my mother wouldn't be here?"

"Honestly, I was hoping she was out, or taking one of her trips out west. I kind of hoped that we'd have the place to ourselves long enough to figure out what to do next."

Torie didn't know how to respond. She was about to argue his points, but at that moment, Wednesday moaned and placed a hand on her very pregnant belly.

"Can we just come in for a minute, just long enough for her to get off her feet and have some water maybe?" Ward asked.

"Yes. Yes, of course," said Torie, ushering them across the threshold and into the living room, where Wednesday plopped down onto the sofa opposite the fireplace. She rubbed her stomach and stretched her legs out.

"Thank you so much," she said. She looked at Torie but quickly broke eye contact when her gaze started to grow hard. "Seriously. I couldn't take another moment cramped up in that car."

"Ward," said Torie, turning to the man she had once made a life with, "what are you doing coming here? You're wanted by the United States government. You've done some really horrible things."

He opened his mouth to reply but stood there slack-jawed, mirroring the look Torie had when she opened the door. His eyes were locked just over her left shoulder.

Torie turned to see Elric, now in his wolf form, stalking up behind her. His ears were flattened back against his head and he sniffed at the air, his yellow eyes locked on Ward.

"That…" began Ward, "that is a seriously big dog you have there." He slowly took a step back, but then froze in place as Elric issued a warning growl. The hair that ran along his spine bristled and raised.

Torie held up a hand in Ward's direction. "Don't move. He won't hurt you. He just doesn't know you." She turned to Elric. "This is Elric. He…makes me feel safe," she said softly.

She reached out with her telepathy. *"Elric. Stop this. You're scaring him."*

No response. The wolf ignored her and continued to stare at Ward. Then, in the space of a heartbeat, he raced across the floor towards the terrified man. Once he was next to Ward, he stopped, sniffed at his leg, and began wagging his tale.

"See," said Torie, trying to control her racing heart, "he's just saying hi."

Ward reached a tentative hand down towards Elric, who again unleashed a warning growl, causing Ward to snatch his hand away.

Then Elric turned away from the man and sniffed Wednesday. The woman didn't draw away and didn't seem afraid.

"Well," she said, reaching out to ruffle the wolf's head, "aren't you the interesting…dog." She shot a glance at Torie and smiled.

"Okay, that's enough playtime," said Torie. "Back into the bedroom with you, Elric," she said, pointing to the back of the house.

Instead of following her lead, the wolf simply huffed, circled around, and then plopped himself in front of the fireplace, curling into a ball.

Ward swallowed hard and slowly moved over to the couch to stand next to Wednesday.

"Jesus, Torie, you never liked dogs before. And now you've gone and gotten the *Hound of the Baskervilles* for a pet."

Elric snorted loudly, his eyes focusing again on Ward.

The man was taken aback, and quickly looked away, focusing on his estranged wife.

"Look, you have every right to hate me," he began.

Torie cut him off with a sharp laugh. "You think?"

Ward nodded. "I deserve that. And so much more. That night, the night I left, I hadn't planned on doing it that way. I thought I'd have a little more time to…extricate myself, in a way that wouldn't hurt you."

"Extricate yourself?" Torie said. "You know, you always treated our marriage like it was some kind of extended business arrangement, so of course you would refer to running out on your family like that."

"I didn't have time to do anything else," he said, his voice rising in tempo as he tried to plead his case. "I…we… got a tip that the feds were on to us and were moving in the next day. We had to run."

Torie looked at him, her feelings turning more and more to anger the longer he sat in front of her. This man had humiliated her, left her and their son, defrauded millions from their community, and then disappeared into the night.

And here he was, sitting in her house, with his pregnant mistress.

Torie felt her anger flare up, and in response, one of the martini glasses on the kitchen island shattered with a pop.

"What was that?" Ward asked, startled.

"Not your business is what that was," said Torie roughly.

Ward settled back into the couch slowly. Wednesday just stared at Torie, the slightest of grins on her lips.

"Where have you been?" asked Torie.

"Driving. Honestly, we had plans to leave the country, to move somewhere that has no extradition agreement with the United Staes."

Torie held up a hand. "No specifics like that. Just because you're going to jail doesn't mean I'm getting dragged in as well for knowing your lame-ass plans. I meant in general. How have they not caught you?"

"I didn't realize just how long they had me under surveillance. The airports were all staked out. My cards and accounts were frozen, everything around me was tapped. All I had was the cash we had managed to keep. We've been on the move, staying at little fleabag motels, paying for everything in cash. I just needed somewhere that I could decompress for a bit; figure out next steps. Wednesday mentioned the town where her mother lived would be perfect, that no one would be able to find us here if we didn't want to be found."

He looked at Torie sheepishly. "Of course, you were the last person I ever thought I'd see here. Given that you and Alva weren't the closest."

Torie had to blink rapidly and banish any thoughts of his tongue exploding in his mouth. How dare he mention her mother's name?

"Where did you think I was going to go, Ward?" Her voice was beginning to tremble, not from sadness, but from barely contained rage. "And not even me...did you think about Shawn at all, and what this might do to him?"

For the first time since walking through her door, Torie saw Ward flinch. He broke eye contact and looked away.

"I left his trust alone. He's well taken care of."

"Well, aren't you just the big man for doing that. Leave him some money as you walk out of his life forever. Because that's what this is, Ward. Forever. There's no coming back from what you've done."

"And you don't think I know that? It wasn't easy."

"No. I think it was that easy for you. Being less than a man was obviously right up your alley." She folded her arms, clenching her fist to try and slow her out-of-control heartbeat.

"How is he? Has he asked about me?"

"You don't get to ask that. You don't get to say you miss him. You don't get to waltz in here and ask about anyone, especially him or my mother..." Hot tears filled her eyes as she finished that sentence.

Ward frowned, picking up on something in her tone. "Torie, where is Alva?"

"She's gone, Ward. She...passed." No way did he deserve to know how she died. She turned away from him, not wanting him to see the pain on her face, and her not wanting to see the shocked look on his.

Before he could say anything, there was a brief knock on the door before it swung open.

Jasmin walked in, rummaging through her purse. "Okay, Torie, what's so import?" Her voice trailed off as she looked up and saw Ward and Wednesday sitting on the couch. "Whoa. What the hell is going on here?"

"Jasmin, this is Ward," Torie offered. "Ward, this is my friend Jasmin."

He made to stand up, extending his hand, but one look from Jasmin's dark eyes made him think better of shaking hands.

"I guess my reputation precedes me," he said softly.

"You could say that," Jasmin said, her voice steel and ice. She looked over at Wednesday and narrowed her eyes. "I know who you are as well."

"Indeed," said Wednesday. "And I know you. Well, at least I feel like I know your spirit."

Ward looked at her curiously. "Why do I get the feeling you know a lot more people in this town than just your mother?"

"Oh, let's just say I can sense a kindred spirit," said Wednesday.

"There is nothing about me that is kindred to you, you gold digging-" Jasmin began, only to be cut off by Ward.

"Hey, that's uncalled for," he said.

Jasmin gave him a look that seemed to stab at his bladder, and for a second, Ward was afraid he would urinate in his pants. He shut up quickly and sank back into the couch.

That was when Jasmin noticed the state Wednesday was in.

"Pregnant? You're pregnant?" she said, shocked.

"Can't hide anything from you, huh?" Wednesday said with a smile. "Must be those acute senses your people are known for." She looked from Jasmin to Torie and smiled again.

Torie looked at her, narrowing her eyes. "You really should have kept in contact with your mother, Wednesday."

The young fae's eyes narrowed. "What is that supposed to mean?"

"Why don't you tell us about the baby, Wednesday?" said Jasmin, before Torie could answer the question. "I mean, it can't be his, right?"

Ward looked confused. "What do you mean it can't be mine?"

"Ward, you told me she wasn't pregnant," said Torie. "And that was only a few months ago. She looks like she's close to term; so how's that possible?"

Ward looked confused, then stood, facing the two witches. "You know what? We obviously made a mistake coming here. I think we should just get going."

He moved to reach for Wednesday, to help her to her feet, when Jasmin stepped forward.

"Go to sleep, Ward," she said in a whisper, waving a hand in front of his face.

Instantly, he dropped onto the sofa, his head tilted to one side as he began to snore.

"Okay, now we can talk," said Jasmin to the fae. "We know what you are, and I'm pretty sure you know who we are. So cut the bullshit and tell us what is going on."

Wednesday snapped at them, her eyes filled with fury. "What happened to my mother? Why isn't she answering my calls?"

"Because she's dead," said Jasmin, her voice sharper than she meant it to be.

Wednesday sank back onto the sofa, her face blank.

"How?" she asked.

"We don't know," said Torie. "We found her face down in her kitchen."

Wednesday's lip quivered. "What were two witches doing in our home?"

"She asked for our help," said Torie. "She was worried that something had happened to you because you cut off communication. So she sought us out to help track you down."

Wednesday let out a long sigh, sitting forward to place her head in her hands, shaking it from side to side.

"She knew not to try and find me. Why would she do that?" She moaned into her hands as her shoulders began to heave, emotions wracking her body. "I told her I would get in touch when it was safe."

"You mean when you and Ward were safely out of the country?" asked Torie.

"No. I mean when it was safe for me to come back home."

"What are you not telling us?" pushed Jasmin. "Why did

you run off with Torie's husband. Whose baby are you carrying?"

"And don't try telling us it's Wards," said Torie. "I know for a fact he's been snipped."

Wednesday looked up at the two of them through red-rimmed eyes.

"It doesn't matter. I'm as good as dead now. I only came back here to get my mother. I told Ward we could lay low here, that no one would find us, but I really just wanted to come get her and take her away with us."

Jasmin narrowed her eyes. "Speak up, and no lies. We can smell a lie." She glanced over at Elric who was watching the fae with rapt attention.

Wednesday snorted. "Does Ward know about you?" she asked Torie. "That his ex-wife is a witch who keeps the company of a werewolf?"

"What I am and who I spend time with is none of your damn business, home-wrecker," replied Torie.

"Maybe if you had spent a little more time making a more welcoming home for Ward, he wouldn't have come to me," Wednesday replied with a huff.

"Why, you little frog," cried Torie, stretching her hand out towards Wednesday. "I hope you burn in hell!"

Before she could stop herself, orange flames danced from Torie's hand, snaking out in Wednesday's direction.

Chapter Seven

Wednesday screamed as orange flames engulfed her. She fell back onto the couch, clutching at her stomach protectively.

"Torie! No!" screamed Jasmin.

Torie brought her outstretched hand to her mouth, horrified at what she had just done. She screamed as well, just as Elric shifted back to his human form and grabbed the throw rug off the floor, ready to toss it on the burning fae.

But then, just as quickly as the flames engulfed her, they began to flicker and die down, turning pale as they evaporated around Wednesday. When they were gone, there was not even smoke to mark their passing, and the young fae was left sitting in shock, looking down at her body. There wasn't a blemish on her; it was as if nothing had happened.

"Jasmin," breathed Torie, "thank you. I didn't mean to do that…I was just so angry."

Jasmin walked slowly over to the fae and examined her. "I didn't do anything."

"Wait, if you didn't put the fire out, then who did?" asked Elric.

Wednesday eyed Torie, her gaze narrow and hard.

"You could have killed me! And my baby!" she shouted. "Ward was right, you are unstable."

"I am so sorry...you have to believe I would never do anything to harm a child. Any child," Torie said, tears flowing from her eyes.

Elric walked over to the fae and sniffed her.

"Ew," she said, drawing back from him. "Can you please put a leash on your dog."

"It was the baby," Elric said. "I don't know how, but I can smell magic coming off her...but it's centered on the baby she's carrying."

Jasmin closed her eyes and stretched out an arm, placing her hand over Wednesday's stomach.

"I think he's right. Somehow, the child protected her from the flames. How is this possible?"

Wednesday looked away, refusing to make eye contact with the women.

"How far along are you?" asked Jasmin.

Wednesday hesitated, and the two women could tell from the look in her eyes that she was debating how much to trust them.

Finally, she huffed, taking a deep breath.

"I don't know. I...this happened a couple of months ago. Just before Ward and I left the city together."

Torie blinked, staring at the woman, thinking maybe she had not heard her correctly.

"I'm sorry, what do you mean a couple of months ago? As in, you were already pregnant then or...?"

"No," said Wednesday. "I wasn't pregnant two and a

half months ago, and now I feel like I'm ready to give birth any day now."

"Whoa," said Jasmin. "What is the typical gestation length for fae?"

"Because we are longer lived than humans, our pregnancies last longer. Typically, thirteen months. This-" she pointed to her belly, "-I can't explain."

"Who is the father?" asked Jasmin. "Is it Ward?"

"No," she replied. "But he thinks it is his."

"What?" cried Torie. "How stupid is he? He's had a vasectomy."

"Yes, I know. I told him that with every medical procedure there is always a chance it didn't take, and he believed that."

"This is what you married?" said Jasmin, pointing to Ward's sleeping form.

Torie shrugged. "Hindsight..." she said, sheepishly. "But I saw you about a month ago, and you weren't showing."

Wednesday nodded. "I was pregnant at the time, but the fetus is growing exceptionally fast. Every instinct I have tells me it's almost time to deliver. That was one of the reasons I was coming home. It was also one of the reasons we couldn't travel. I told Ward it wouldn't be safe for the baby; and that's true."

"So didn't he at least question why it was growing so fast?" asked Jasmin.

"He did. I said that happens with some women; that the mother doesn't show until just before the baby is born."

"Jesus," said Jasmin, shaking her head. "Not the sharpest tool in the shed."

"I told him I hid the pregnancy from him most of the

time because I didn't want him to feel pressured to leave his marriage." She stopped, looking over at Torie.

"So he really did want to leave on his own," Torie said.

Wednesday didn't answer. She didn't have to.

"Oh bloody hell..." said Wednesday, looking over their shoulder towards the kitchen threshold.

Jasmin and Torie turned to see Fionna, in her squirrel form, on the kitchen floor staring intently at them.

She shifted to her human form and walked into the room.

"What's going on and who are these people?" she asked.

"That," said Jasmin, pointing to Ward, "is Torie's ex, and this is the trick who stole him."

Fionna's eyes narrowed and she stepped aggressively towards Wednesday, one hand drawn back.

"Why you trashy-" She started, open hand ready to deliver a slap.

Elric stepped gently between them, trying to deescalate the situation.

"Easy there," he said to Fionna. "She's in a delicate way."

Fionna saw her stomach and slowly lowered her hand. Wednesday smiled and rubbed her belly.

"Please let her stay," said Fionna, turning to Torie. "Because that way, once she delivers her spawn, she can take an ass whooping like the grown-ass fae-hussy she is."

"Hussy?" said Wednesday, rolling her eyes. "I had forgotten how quaint and trapped in time this town is. Welcome back to Mayberry." Her voice trailed off as she dropped onto the couch.

"And she's not staying here," said Jasmin. "Or have you forgotten she and Ward are wanted fugitives? If they get caught here, it's your ass as well as theirs." She leveled a hard gaze at Torie, who nodded

"I know. And I don't want them here either."

Wednesday gasped, grabbing at her stomach and taking deep breaths, stretching her legs out and moaning. "Whew. That was a big one. Baby He or She is kicking up a storm. I don't think it will be long now." She looked up, eyes wide, searching for a sympathetic face.

Torie and Jasmin crossed their arms, regarding her with something that approached disdain.

"Bitch please," said Jasmin. "I don't care if that thing you're carrying starts carving its way out of you like a reverse Jack-O-Lantern. I'm not boiling a pot of water or getting clean linen to assist. You want help? Start giving us the answers we need."

Wednesday exhaled sharply, looking at the three women and the werewolf.

"Fine. I knew Ward couldn't have any more children. I could sense it when we met. But you have to understand something about fae; we all have a biological imperative to reproduce. We can do it by choice of course, but for those of us who do not...we fall into what you might call 'heat' once every couple of decades.

"A few months ago, it was my time. I fought it as long as I could, but there is no resisting the call. It's a built-in drive to make sure our race survives. All female fae have to give birth. Knowing that Ward could not give me a child, I returned to Singing Falls."

"Wait," said Jasmin, "you steal Torie's husband, then slink off from him to hook up with someone else to have a baby? You are so foul."

"I don't expect you to understand. It may not seem palatable to humans, but I had no choice in the matter. I was driven. It was as if a fever had taken me over. I felt commanded to return here, to find a fae mate, but instead, I met another."

"Another what?" said Torie. "A shifter? Vampire? Human? Who or what fathered your baby?"

"I thought he was a human. But it turned out he possessed a magic that I didn't know men possessed."

"The man-witch," Torie said, looking at Jasmin and Fionna. "I'll fill you in later. Keep going, Wednesday. Where did you meet him?"

"The Jack Hole, that dive bar on the outskirts of town. The one that caters to humans who like to mix it up with supernaturals from time to time."

Jasmin wrinkled her nose, turning to Torie. "It's a bar where curious humans go to meet up with paranormals. They consider it taking a walk on the wild side."

"It's a disgusting place. Figures you would be there," Fionna said, practically spitting the words at Wednesday.

"Like I said, I was drawn. And since we are all being so open, I hoped to find a human that could fulfill my needs; preferably one that looked like Ward, in order to allay any suspicion down the road. I don't know why; I just knew this was something I needed to do."

Torie felt a twitch in her eye and had to remind herself that flambéing the gloating woman who stood before her wasn't an option.

"But when I saw this man, when I felt the touch of his magic, I knew he was the one. I would have a child that was half fae and half witch. We didn't even talk. We both knew what was going to happen. I followed him out of the bar, and well…this is the result."

Fionna narrowed her eyes and made a disgusted,

clicking sound with her mouth before turning away from the fae.

"But I thought it would be a normal gestation," said Wednesday. "I didn't expect...this."

"And what about the man who impregnated you?" questioned Torie. "Where is he now? Did you stay in touch?"

Wednesday shook her head. "I knew instantly I was pregnant. So I left him that night, sneaking out of the hotel room he had rented, and heading back up to New York."

"Christ," said Jasmin. "You are absolute trash. And now your trashy ass has possibly set us on a collision path with a warlock." She turned to Jasmin.

"Yes. Elric knew a lot more about them than we did. Including how they gain their magic, which is pretty perverse and dangerous for us."

She asked Elric to relay what he had told her earlier.

Fionna was the first to speak up. "Do you think this warlock is somehow tied to, or involved with, whoever sent Breonna to kill all those shifters?"

"It's been in the back of my mind," said Jasmin. "Breonna said she was collecting certain organs and parts off the shifters for whoever she was working for. She didn't know why. Now it's starting to make a little more sense."

"How?" said Elric.

"You said yourself that warlocks feed off the magical source of other paranormals...witches in particular," said Jasmin. "Well, what if it's not only witches they can use?"

"The shifters," said Torie.

"Yes. Maybe this warlock is trying something new."

"Did this warlock kill my mother?" asked Wednesday, her voice cold and flat.

"We don't know," said Torie, "but your mother did say

she was approached by a male witch who claimed he could help her locate you. That was the last we heard from her."

A groan from Ward interrupted their dialog. He moaned and shifted his weight, making an effort to sit up.

Quickly, Elric and Fionna shifted back into their animal forms.

Ward's eyes fluttered open, focusing on the room around him. "What…what happened?"

"Honey, you said you needed to close your eyes just for a minute, and the next thing we knew you were snoring. The drive up here, and the stress of everything is finally catching up to you." Wednesday poured on the concern as she reached over and stroked his forehead lovingly.

Torie frowned. Lies rolled off this woman's lips way too easily. She disliked her immediately, but now she also distrusted her.

"Yeah, I guess. I just don't remember falling asleep. That's never happened before." He froze in place as his gaze locked on Elric and Fionna. "Is that…a squirrel sitting there. With your giant dog?"

Torie nodded, not taking her eyes off Ward.

"So what, this is like some kind of animal sanctuary or something?" he asked, mostly in jest.

"What it is," Torie said, "is not your concern."

Ward flinched. "I guess it's a good thing Alva isn't around. I bet she would just love you having a bunch of creatures running around her house."

Torie felt her anger try to flare up again. The nerve of this man insinuating that he knew what her mother would and would not like,

"I think you would be the only creature she'd be sad to see I have around. She left the house to me. So that means if I want to have one of everything that walks these woods in my house, I can. As a matter of fact, no matter what animal I had under this roof, I can guarantee they will treat me better than you did."

He stood, the muscles of his jaw clenching. Elric rose as well, the hackles along his back rising as he moved closer to Torie.

"C'mon Wednesday, we need to go," he reached his hand behind him, waiting for her to take it. She moved slowly, glancing up at Torie with pleading eyes.

"Wait," said Torie, looking at Wednesday and not Ward. "It's late, and you don't know these roads. Plus...Wednesday looks like she needs to be off her feet for a bit." She took a deep breath. "Why don't you stay until the morning? At least you can shower and get a decent night's sleep. Wouldn't want you suddenly dozing off again while driving and carrying your precious cargo."

Her tone was biting and elicited a slight chuckle from Jasmin.

Ward looked closely at her. "Why are you suddenly being nice to me?"

"I'm not. I'm being nice to her unborn child. But not you, Ward; let's keep that straight."

Wednesday stood, making her way over to Torie to say thank you. As she moved, her white blouse shifted, revealing a silver key necklace.

"What an interesting necklace," said Torie. "Where did you get it?"

"Oh this," said Wednesday, fingering the silver piece. "It was a gift to me and my mother. I'm not sure what it opens, but mother said it would come in handy one day."

"Who gave it to your mother?" asked Jasmin.

"I don't remember her name. She's the secretary to the

neighborhood vamp-" She caught herself and stopped. "Man that runs the law office in town."

"Arnold?" questioned Torie. "Arnold gave it to your mother?"

"Yes. Why?"

Torie didn't answer, but instead looked at Jasmin, eyes wide.

Why would the vampire who had tried to kill them, give a set of silver keys to a fae and her daughter? Torie looked down at Fionna. The squirrel looked back, her black eyes flashed red, and she bared her teeth before running through the kitchen and out the back door.

Tomorrow was going to be one hell of an interesting day.

Chapter Eight

The next morning, Torie was in the kitchen making a pan of scrambled eggs. Bacon was in the stove, and a fresh pot of coffee was brewing.

Wednesday entered looking refreshed and offered Torie an awkward smile, unable to make eye contact. She opened her mouth to speak but was cut off when Torie raised her hand.

"Before you say anything, let me apologize for my behavior last night. I shouldn't have done that to you...the whole fire thing. Truthfully, I let my anger get the best of me. It wasn't directed at you. I wasn't married to you."

Wednesday nodded, pouring herself a cup of coffee. She stopped before raising it to her lips and looked at Torie.

"I'm sorry. May I have a cup of your coffee?"

Torie nodded and went back to stirring the eggs.

"I should apologize as well. I goaded you into reacting the way you did. I shouldn't have." She eased herself onto one of the barstools, watching and savoring the smell of bacon. "That smells amazing. I haven't had anything that wasn't served in a fast-food wrapper in weeks."

Torie frowned. "That can't be good for the baby."

Wednesday shrugged. "We didn't really have a choice. I guess looking back on things, this wasn't planned out too well."

"Whose idea was the plan?" queried Torie. "The pyramid scheme I mean?"

"It was Ward's. I mean, I was fully onboard with it, but he came up with the initial details. We were only going to do it for a while; just long enough to get the company out of a financial jam we were in. But then, when he saw how much money we were bringing in and able to keep by not reinvesting it…it just kind of grew to the point that eventually we didn't know how to stop it."

Torie stared at her, wondering if she could believe the fae.

"Our lawyer said it was your idea. From what he could tell by the way things had been structured."

"I let Ward set it up so that it pointed to me. I figured that if…when…we got caught, I'd be able to return to good ole Singing Falls and disappear. Good luck to the feds trying to locate a fae in the woods of a supernatural community." She was quiet, sipping at her coffee.

"So what changed?" asked Torie, fearing the response. "Other than the obvious that is." She eyed Wednesday's growing stomach.

The fae gave Torie an unblinking look. "I fell in love with a human."

Torie nodded, moving to the cabinet to remove a plate. She set it in front of the fae and heaped eggs onto it before turning to take a pan of bacon out of the stove.

"So, you're really in love with Ward?"

Wednesday swallowed hard. "I am. I didn't intend that, I swear. I should have never left Singing Falls. My mother said it would be the end of me. But I just...I wanted to see and experience something outside of this town. And I fell in love with the luxuries that money could buy. Once you've experienced heated marble floors...there's no going back to tree houses and rooms heated by a single, tiny fireplace."

Torie didn't say anything. For her, she was experiencing the opposite.

She had spent the majority of her life living in the lap of luxury. She had been surrounded by creature comforts that most people would have gladly given a limb to experience. But it had all felt empty in the long run. A huge house filled with fine things could still feel incredibly lonely and cold.

She hadn't realized just how numb she was becoming until she moved to Singing Falls and into her mother's house. There was a definite difference between a house and a home; and now she could honestly say she was home.

At least until her sense of peace was cut short by her estranged ex and his mistress.

"So, not that it's my business, but if you love him so much, why are you constantly lying to him? Trust me, you're sowing seeds that will bloom into a cancerous growth down the road."

Wednesday looked at her, her forkful of eggs paused midway to her mouth. "What am I supposed to say? That I'm from a race of supernatural creatures he doesn't even know are real? That I live in a community filled with other paranormal creatures? That I am carrying the spawn of a magical being that impregnated me only a couple months ago?"

Torie arched a single eyebrow. "Sounds to me like

you've been giving this a lot of thought. But for what it's worth…if you truly love him, then yes. Tell him the truth."

"And what about you? Are you going to tell him that you're a witch and you're playing house with a werewolf?"

Torie narrowed her eyes. "My truth is for me to know right now. He is no longer a part of my life; and I don't owe him jack shit."

They stared at one another; each refusing to break the other's gaze. The tension in the room was cut by the man in question as he strolled into the kitchen, stretching both arms over his head.

"Wow, Torie, that guest room mattress is like a cloud from heaven. I didn't realize how much I needed a good night's rest." He looked around, reading the temperature of the room. "Did I miss something?"

"Not at all," said Torie. "I was just telling Wednesday how important nutrition was for the baby. She's eating for two now."

"Oh yeah. Hey, remember how you blew up with Shawn? You were the size of a house." He chuckled. "Oh that looks awesome. How about you slide me some of those eggs?"

"Sorry," said Torie, taking the pan of eggs and scraping the rest onto Wednesday's plate. "She's eating for two, remember?"

Ward frowned. "Yes, of course. But what about that bacon…"

Torie took the sheet pan from the top of the stove and walked around the island towards Ward. Then, she kept going, moving past him to the garbage can and dumped the meat into it.

"Sorry. I don't believe in encouraging cannibalism in this house."

"Huh?" was all he could say, looking forlornly at the garbage.

A scraping noise, followed by some high-pitched squeaking caught his attention before he could protest, causing him to look around the room.

There, by the back patio, was Fionna in squirrel form, sitting next to Elric. Torie walked through the workroom and opened the French doors, letting them both into the house.

"Oh great," said Ward. "The menagerie returns. Wait…is that squirrel dragging a…stake?"

Torie looked and sure enough, Fionna had whittled a stick into the form of a long stake, which she dragged with her into the house.

"What?" asked Torie, walking over to the squirrel. "Don't be ridiculous, Ward. She's obviously just been chewing on a stick, that's all." She bent down and picked up the stake, tossing it out the door. "Why in the world would a squirrel have a stake?" She gave Fionna a look and then turned back to the guests in the room.

"I have to run an errand this morning," she said, giving Wednesday a knowing look. "I shouldn't be gone long."

"Well, we will probably be gone by the time you get back," said Ward, scratching his head.

Torie pursed her lips, giving them both a long look.

"Stay for lunch," she said. "At least that way it will give you time to think about what you need to do next and make some concrete plans. You can't keep dragging a pregnant woman all over creation. Especially one that looks like she could give birth at any moment."

She wasn't exaggerating. To her eyes, Wednesday looked even bigger than she had last night.

"Where are you going?" asked Wednesday pointedly. "Should I go?"

"No. You should stay here until we work everything out. I'm going to call my friend Jasmin to join me. But you stay here." She turned to Ward. "Needless to say, you probably shouldn't leave the house."

"Yeah fine," he said absent-mindedly as he moved over to the refrigerator and began rummaging through it.

Wednesday followed Torie as she walked out of the kitchen into the living room.

"Why shouldn't I go?" she whispered. "If you're doing something to find out what happened to my mother, I should be there."

"Look," said Torie, "a lot has happened in this town in the last couple of months. Someone, or something, took control of Arnold and made him kill a lot of shifters in town. He's fine now...or at least I think he is. We were able to stop him, but we still don't know who was pulling the strings in the background. That means there is still a supernatural killer out there. A killer who may or may not have killed your mother."

"All the more reason I should go," said Wednesday forcefully.

"And do what? You're pregnant," answered Torie, "and that baby should be your priority right now."

Wednesday studied Torie's eyes. "You think the warlock has something to do with all of this, don't you?"

"Jasmin does. And I trust her instincts. It's just a little too coincidental that you were impregnated by a warlock and had contact with Arnold when he was under the mental control of...something. I don't believe in coincidence; so yes, I think there is a connection here, somewhere."

"Why do you care?" asked Wednesday. "This isn't your

community. You weren't born here. Why do you care about what happens here?"

Torie regarded her. "You're right, I wasn't born here. But *you* were. So I think the question should be; why don't *you* care?"

There was a knock on the door, and Torie moved to open it, smiling as Jasmin stepped through.

"Jasmin," said Wednesday, in a dry tone.

"Whore," said Jasmin, brushing past her as she headed for the kitchen.

Torie rolled her eyes as she and Wednesday followed Jasmin into the kitchen. Ward was sitting at the island eating a Greek yogurt that he had found in the back of the fridge.

"You're still here?"

"Oh, Jasmin, right?" said Ward. "It's nice to see you again. Torie said she was calling you, but I didn't think you'd get here so fast. Or...are you the maid? Am I in the way of your cleaning?"

Jasmin's eyes flared. "You know, you're looking very sleepy again..."

"No!" said Torie, stepping in front of her friend. "Ward had a good night's sleep and will be hanging out here until we get back from out errand." She gave Jasmin a nod, her eyes pleading with her friend. "You know...that errand we have to run."

"Oh, I know the errand," said Jasmin, glancing at Wednesday once again.

"And, Ward," said Torie, "she is not my maid. She is my friend. And if you insult her like that again, I'll call the feds on you myself."

Just then, the front door opened once again and Fionna walked in. She breezed into the kitchen and stood next to Wednesday.

"Hello, Fionna," Wednesday said.

"Hi, trash," she replied, ignoring her to focus on Torie. "So, are we ready?"

"Hello," said Ward, offering a hand toward the shifter. "Have we met?"

"Yes. Though you looked better passed out on the couch last night when I stopped by."

Ward withdrew his hand, taking a deep breath and exhaling audibly. "Seems like everyone here has already made their minds up about me."

Fionna continued to ignore him, smiling instead at Torie. "Are you okay? How are you holding up?"

"I'm fine, Fionna," Torie said. "Are you sure you want to come with us? I mean, Jasmin and I are perfectly fine running this particular errand."

"I'm fine. I could do with a little errand running. I promise I'll be good."

She nodded and headed for the door, motioning for Elric to follow her. He trotted along, wagging his tale gleefully.

"Oh, um, I was thinking that maybe Elric would stay here. You know how he likes guarding the house," said Torie.

"Oh no, I get the feeling he wants to go as well," said Fionna. "You never know when he might be needed. On an errand run I mean. Besides, you know he doesn't like strangers in your house. Who knows what he might do if left alone with your…friends."

Torie frowned and nodded. "Fine. Just let me get my purse." She headed for her bedroom at the back of the house before turning and beckoning Wednesday. "Oh, could you join me for a second?"

The fae followed her from the kitchen into her bedroom.

"You don't have to worry. I'll make sure Ward stays in the house."

"Like I care what he does. I need your necklace."

Wednesday took it off and handed it over to the witch who slipped it into her purse.

"Torie, if you find out that Arnold had something to do with my mother being killed, I want you to let me know."

Torie looked at her but didn't answer.

"Cos if he did, I don't care how pregnant I am; I'm staking his undead ass."

Torie nodded. In her mind, she thought of Fionna, and knew that there was a good chance Wednesday would have to get in line for that honor.

Chapter Nine

"Okay, first things first," said Torie as they sped towards town. "No one kills anyone, agreed?"

Jasmin was riding shotgun next to Torie and made it a point to look at her and then into the backseat at Fionna and Elric, before placing a hand dramatically on her chest.

"I know you're not talking to me," she said. "I'm not the one who tried to barbecue my ex-husband's hooker while she was sitting on the couch."

Torie pursed her lips. "I have already apologized for that. And no, I wasn't talking about you." She glanced into the rearview mirror before cutting her eyes back to the road.

"Then if you're talking about them, you need to address them directly," replied Jasmin. "Hmph...I can control myself. I not going to go around just killing people for no reason."

"If you're talking about me, I can agree to that to a point," said Fionna.

"What do you mean?" asked Torie.

"What I mean is, I'm fine unless he bares his fangs or

snaps at us, or looks at us funny, or...wait, does he have fangs yet? I mean, you ripped them out by the roots if I remember correctly."

Torie shifted her weight in the car seat. "I have no idea."

"His fangs have regrown...for the most part," said Jasmin. "Though he's not happy with the way they came in."

"Why are you still hanging out with him?" asked Fionna. "He killed my best friend. Taylor was your friend as well." The words came out sharper than she intended.

"I'm not hanging out with him. But I do check in on him and Eddie from time to time. Eddie is still recovering, and I want to make sure he isn't slipping health-wise."

"You mean you want to make sure he hasn't been turned into a human Capri Sun pouch," said Fionna.

Jasmin snapped around and stared at the shifter but didn't say anything.

"You know, that says a lot," said Torie. "The fact Eddie was attacked and nearly killed by Arnold, but has not only forgiven him but given him a second chance. He loves Arnold and knows that he was not in control of himself when he committed those atrocities. If he can do that, then maybe we can forgive as well."

"You know, statistically speaking, Fionna is probably right," said Elric.

"About what?" asked Torie.

"About the chances that Arnold will probably try to drain Eddie. Vampires have a survival urge that surpasses even that of werewolves. But more importantly, there identity and their ability to thrive, is wrapped up in their fangs. If Arnold is truly weakened and has lost his most powerful weapons, his fangs, then his most base survival instincts may kick in at some point…"

"So what are you saying…that if you were in his place, and Torie was in Eddie's place, you'd…"

"Never," said Elric. "That would not happen. A wolf's instincts for self-preservation only goes so far. We might chew our own limb off to escape a trap, but we would never hurt a mate. Not under any conditions."

Torie blushed a deep crimson, gripping the wheel a little tighter.

"You don't like that?" Elric said, his body language suddenly mimicking Torie's.

Part of her loved the sentiment of what he said, but she didn't particularly care for the way it was said.

"No, I actually find it very comforting," Torie said. "It's just that, well, the term 'mate'; it has a connotation in my mind…"

"She means it sounds so carnal," said Jasmin, grinning from ear to ear.

Elric was quiet for a moment before speaking up. "I think, at some point in life, we outgrow calling another adult a boyfriend or a girlfriend. But I can see where mate might not be the right term either. Especially since we haven't fully consummated our relationship."

Torie felt her crimson deepen. She knew he didn't mean anything by it, but his bluntness was something she was still trying to get used to.

"Wait," said Jasmin, "you two haven't yet-"

"Not your business, Jasmin," said Torie, ignoring her friend as she threw back her head in laughter.

Fionna leaned forward in the car. "Wait. So what I want to know is; what does he mean by haven't *fully* consummated the relationship?"

"Okay that's enough of that," said Torie, speaking quickly because she was afraid Elric might actually elaborate. "There are other things we should be talking about; like what exactly are we going to say to Arnold to let us into a safe-deposit box that doesn't belong to us?"

Jasmin rubbed at her chin, deep in thought, before turning to Torie. "That's a good question. You know what a better one is? What is going through your head now with your ex in your house?" she asked, before looking over her shoulder at Elric. "And how are you doing with it?"

For once, Torie was anxious to hear how Elric would answer that. She had refrained from reaching into his mind while he had been in his wolf form. She respected his privacy in this situation and knew that if he were having a problem with Ward being in the house, he would speak up.

At least, she hoped he would.

Elric seemed to consider how to answer this and measured his words carefully.

"If you are asking if I'm threatened by the man who shared a large part of his life with Torie; no, I am not. Am I uncomfortable that he is in her house? Perhaps a little."

Torie felt like someone had just punched her in the stomach.

"Elric, why?" she asked.

"For the same reason I mentioned; he is someone you have a very long history with. You know one another in a way that no one else does. And you have raised a child together."

"You have a point," Torie replied. "But do you know what it feels like when you realize, after so many years with someone, that they are not the person you thought you knew? That they are, in fact, a traitor to your life together? That's what it feels like to be betrayed on the level that

Ward betrayed me. I feel like he cheated on my entire life." She felt a single tear drop from her eye, and she quickly reached up to wipe it away.

Jasmin reached over and rubbed the back of her neck and shoulders with one hand. "I'm sorry for bringing that up. I just needed to make sure you were okay."

"I am," she answered. "It's weird, when all of this first happened, I had fantasies of what I would say to Ward if I ever saw him again. It warmed my heart to imagine how it would feel to slap him in his smirking face, and then follow that up with a severe cussing."

"Oh, did you do that?" asked Fionna.

"No. Somewhere along the way, over the past few months, I've let go of that anger. When I saw him, I was shocked, but the anger wasn't there. To be honest, I felt nothing for him." She glanced in the mirror again at Elric. "I don't have any feelings for him anymore."

"I know that," said Elric. "Still, I don't like him being in your house. Mostly because you can get into a lot of trouble harboring him. I would hate to see you carted off to jail when we are just getting to know one another."

The look of surprise that crossed Torie's face made her friends laugh.

"Wait, are you saying the only reason you don't like having him in the house is because you're worried about the legal consequences?"

Elric nodded, an ear-to-ear grin breaking out on his face.

"Why didn't you just say that?" asked Torie.

"Maybe I wanted to see what you would say."

Jasmin nodded her head, smiling at Elric before looking at Torie. "You know, I like this one."

"Well, I don't like him," said Fionna. "He smells funny. And I certainly don't like that fae either."

Torie frowned. "Yeah. That's a tough one. I have to say, I'm not a fan of her either. But she's pregnant, and as much as I'd like to, I can't see myself throwing her out in the street."

"I'll do it for you," said Fionna. "As big as she is, I doubt she can put up much of a fight."

Torie laughed. "I told her she needs to come clean with Ward. About the baby I mean." She relayed her morning conversation with Wednesday to her passengers.

"That's crazy," said Jasmin. "Ward really thinks she is carrying his baby?"

"And she lies so easily to him," said Torie.

"Do you think she'll tell him the truth?" asked Fionna.

"Don't know. Honestly, I'm not even sure I care at this point," replied Torie. "Even after everything she said, I feel bad for her."

"Why?" said Fionna. "She is deliberately deceiving someone. She stole him away from you, then cheated on him with some magic man in order to get knocked up. And why? Because...hormones? Whatever. I don't know what the female equivalent of not being able to keep it in your pants is, but she has it."

"Fionna!" said Jasmin. "We don't judge, you know that."

Fionna crossed her arms and sank back into the car seat.

"She's not wrong," said Elric. "Fae are tricky creatures. It's true that when their heat overtakes them, they are driven to reproduce. But she lied when she said she didn't know when it would happen. Fae can control their cycles... they only come into heat when they allow it."

Fionna and Jasmin stared at him. Torie gripped the wheel harder, gritting her teeth.

"Are you saying that this bitch-" Fionna started.

"Fionna!" said Jasmin, cutting her off.

"Sorry. Are you saying this *fae* came into heat on purpose and then sought out a warlock to seal the deal with?"

Elric nodded.

"You know, I don't think I like you knowing so much about the reproductive proclivities of fae," said Torie, furrowing her brow.

"Torie told me you know a lot about supernaturals," said Jasmin. "She wasn't lying. What about their gestation? Is it normal for a baby to grow that fast?"

"Now that I do not know," said Elric. "But that baby is filled with magic. That much I can tell you. And that isn't normal. Fae, like most magical paranormals, have an affinity for magic, but they aren't steeped in it; not the way this child is. Other than evasion, they don't have a use for magic. But that child reeks of powerful magics."

"That would explain why your fire blast didn't cook them," said Jasmin.

Torie blushed again at the memory of her behavior. "That can never happen again. I was out of control and I'm sorry for that."

"Don't fret," said Jasmin, turning to look out her window. "We've all been there before."

Something in her voice told Torie she didn't want to talk about it, and she would respect that. At least in that moment.

Turning the car into the parking lot of the law offices that Arnold ran, she gave Fionna one last look in the rearview mirror, silently pleading for her to keep her cool.

Like most of the businesses in the small town, the offices were on the main floors of a large corner Victorian. The two floors above it were private residences, typically belonging to the business owner. In this case, the owner residence was located below ground in the basement level. Far away from the North Carolina sunlight that streamed through the upper windows of the building.

There was no one else in the parking lot as they eased into a space right in front of the building. As they exited the car, Jasmin turned to Fionna and held out her hand.

"Let's have it," she said to the shifter.

Fionna rolled her eyes and huffed, before reaching into her jacket and removing a wooden stake from its inner pocket. She handed it over to Jasmin dramatically.

Jasmin tossed it into the front seat before turning to give Fionna the once over. Satisfied she had no more weapons, she ushered them up the white steps to the porch and then the large wooden and glass door that faced them. A sign had been placed on the door stating that the offices were temporarily closed. A telephone number was printed in block letters instructing anyone with an emergency to call.

"What in the world would be considered a legal emergency?" asked Torie.

Jasmin shrugged. "Oh I don't know...maybe a fae mother whose daughter disappeared only to turn up pregnant at the hands of a warlock."

Fionna huffed. "Please. It wasn't his hands that did that to her."

Torie glanced at her friend, trying to stifle a laugh. *Now is not the time for joking*, she reminded herself.

Jasmin pressed the buzzer, and they waited for someone to answer.

"Maybe he's not home," said Fionna. "We should just

go." She turned, heading for the steps that would lead her back to the car, when a creaking signaled the opening of the door.

Eddie opened the door and smiled at his old friends.

"Hello, Jasmin," he said, giving the witch a hug. He turned, greeting Torie, Fionna and Elric in kind. "Come on in. Arnold's been expecting you."

Expecting us, thought Torie, broadcasting her thoughts to Elric.

"Was it just me," whispered Fionna, "or did he say that like he was expecting us for dinner? Only we're the main course?"

The door closed behind them as they entered the vampire's home. Immediately they were engulfed in darkness. A chill ran down Torie's back as a voice penetrated the darkness from somewhere in front of them.

"Ah...hello, Torie," came Arnold's raspy voice. "I've been waiting for this moment."

Chapter Ten

Panicked, Torie instinctively reached for her magic, calling it up, ready to strike out in panic in the general direction from which the vampire's voice came.

She was stopped as the room was suddenly engulfed in blue light emanating from a ball of energy that floated in front of Jasmin. She extended one arm forward, her hand palm out as she commanded the light to shine brighter.

Arnold stood in front of her, dressed in black silk pajamas, he held one arm up to shield his eyes as he backed away from Jasmin. Looking around, Torie could see that Elric had shifted into a truly frightening hybrid wolf form. He still stood upright but his facial features had taken on those of a wolf. His hands were outstretched at his side, inch-long talons protruding from his fingers.

On his shoulder sat Fionna, fully shifted, her eyes blazing red as she regarded the vampire before them.

"Whoa, easy there Jas...I'm not going to hurt anyone," said Arnold.

Eddie quickly jumped between them, using his body to shield his vampire lover.

"He's telling the truth. He's in complete control of himself." He held up his hands, pleading for Jasmin to dim her light.

She did, allowing the blinding blue to flicker down to little more than ambient mood lighting.

"What the hell, Arnold?" she said. "What are you doing skulking around in the dark like that?"

"I'm a vampire, Jasmin," he replied, "skulking is what we do. Since when do you come loaded for bear like that?"

Fionna leapt off Elric's shoulder, shifting back to human. "Maybe since you killed our friends."

"Fair enough," said the vampire. "I will never be able to apologize to you enough for what I did. I know that."

"Arnold," said Jasmin, "what's with the spooky greeting? And that weird, 'I've been waiting for you, Torie' nonsense?"

"What do you mean? I have been waiting for her. I owe her my life and, even though she didn't have to, I want to thank her for sparing me."

"Wait," said Eddie, "let me get the lights."

He moved to one wall and flipped a few switches, turning on the warm, overhead lighting from a chandelier that hung in the middle of the entry space.

"We get so used to the darkness, we forget to turn them on when company calls," he said.

Looking around, Torie could see the windows had all been covered with blackout drapes that prevented any daylight from entering the space. As her eyes adjusted, she could see that the inside of the house was falling into disrepair. There was peeling paint on the walls here and there, the chandelier itself had more than a few cobwebs forming on the teardrop light bulbs, and the floor looked like it hadn't seen a broom in sometime.

"You don't have to thank me," said Torie, turning her attention back to Arnold. "I'm not a killer."

Jasmin looked at Fionna, cutting off her words before she could utter them.

"Um, Arnold, what's going on with this place? You've always kept it spotless. The last time I was here, it was immaculate," said Jasmin.

"That was a couple of months ago, when I first came back home," said Arnold, looking around. "I just haven't felt much like myself for a while. But," he glanced at Eddie, "I'm getting there. The old Arnold will be back soon enough."

"I hope not," Fionna mumbled under her breath.

Arnold looked at her and started to speak but thought better of it. Instead he just smiled at her, which to Fionna was worse than anything he might have said.

"Arnold, how are you doing?" asked Jasmin. "I mean, as far as…healing goes."

"It's slower than I would have imagined. For a creature who can heal a cut, or even a broken bone, in seconds…this was not the kind of injury any of my kind have ever sustained." He glanced at Torie and gave her a half smile. "Honestly, the mental anguish I still put myself through on a daily basis, over what I did, is more painful than my physical ailments."

"Are you able to feed?" asked Elric.

Torie frowned. Subtlety wasn't his strong suit.

"Not yet," said Arnold. "My fangs are growing back in, but they are not quite in the same position as they were. It will take some getting used to. And I must confess, I'm not that anxious to use them again." His voice trailed off, and Eddie stepped in, clearing his throat.

"He subsist on blood from the blood banks. It's enough to sustain him for as long as needed."

"Until...?" said Elric.

"Until he can feed off animals again," said Fionna, her voice hard and direct.

"Livestock," said Arnold. "And I don't drain them. Cows are large enough that they hardly miss the blood I take from them."

"How are you getting blood from the blood banks?" asked Fionna. "It's not like you can just waltz into a clinic or hospital and ask for a bag of O-negative."

Arnold and Eddie exchanged glances.

"We have help," said Arnold. "We can just leave it at that."

Fionna nodded, and Torie could see her making mental notes.

"Um, Arnold," she said, breaking the tension between he and the shifter, "as much as we wish it were different, we aren't here on a social call."

"Yes, I figured as much," he said. "What can I help you with?"

Torie reached into her purse and removed Wednesday's necklace.

"We need access to the box this key goes to."

He reached into his pocket and took out a white, silken handkerchief. He held out his hand for Torie to drop it into the cloth, where he examined it closely.

Looking up, he noticed they were staring at him.

"It's made of silver," he explained. "It is an uncomfortable metal for vampires to handle."

Jasmin nodded. "Can you show us what it opens?"

Arnold handed the key back to Torie. "There are two of them. The box can't be opened with only one key."

"Well then, it's a good thing I have the other one as well," said Torie, taking out the one that belonged to Wednesday's mother.

"No excuses now," said Jasmin. "I know these go to the security boxes that you provide for your clients. We'd like to open it."

"I don't think that will be possible," said Arnold. "These keys are coded to the specific bio-rhythms of the supernatural they are fashioned for. If I am not mistaken, these were meant for fae; not witches. The box will not open for you."

"Why don't you leave that to us," said Jasmin, stealing a glance at Torie.

Arnold still seemed hesitant and Torie moved to stand next to him, putting a hand on his arm. He flinched at the contact, and she withdrew, sensing his discomfort.

"Arnold, the fae woman I took this from is dead. She reached out to us to help her find her missing daughter. Someone that disappeared in the world of man, not here in Singing Falls. We found her dead in her home yesterday, and we have reason to believe that what happened to her was no accident. This necklace could help us with clues as to what is going on."

He regarded her in silence for a moment. "You have two keys. Is the daughter dead as well?"

"No," she replied. She wasn't sure how much she wanted to reveal at this moment. "She isn't dead, but she isn't in any condition to come here in person."

"That's a shame," said Arnold. "She could have opened it. Or at least given her permission for you to look in the box. You know it's against the law for me to let someone else open it without permission. It would be like a doctor letting you see the medical chart of a friend of yours without their permission."

"We understand that, Arnold," said Jasmin. "And many of the paranormals in this community, myself included, thank you for the privacy you have always maintained in dealing with our affairs; but this could be tied to everything that happened...before."

She glanced at Torie, her gaze matching her words, soft and pleading.

Torie nodded, agreeing with what her friend had said. She hoped she wouldn't have to pull the, "you owe me your life" card, but she was prepared to if that was what it took.

Arnold took a deep breath and looked over at Eddie. The other man nodded and smiled, agreeing with what the witches had said.

"Just this once," said Arnold. "I will allow you a few minutes with the box. But only because I don't believe you can open it, even with the keys. Follow me."

They fell into line behind the vampire and headed down a long hallway that led to a set of back stairs that descended into darkness. Arnold flipped a switch, lighting a set of wall sconces that followed the stairway downward, opening to a large parlor room complete with velvet furniture. Built-in bookcases lined three walls, each stuffed with tomes with their spines facing outward.

Eddie and Elric brought up the rear. Elric had returned to his human form and stopped when Eddie placed a hand on his shoulder.

"Arnold isn't the only one who wants to say thank you. I wanted to thank you and Max as well. You found me that day, when I was close to death up in the mountains. Thank you for taking me back to Torie's house. You saved my life."

Elric smiled. "You don't have to thank me. It was the

right thing to do, and honestly, it would never have occurred to me to do anything differently that day."

Eddie smiled and nodded, giving the werewolf's hand a firm shake as he walked to the center of the room to stand next to Arnold.

"So where is the vault you keep everything in?" asked Torie.

"You're standing in it," replied Arnold, gesturing to the space around him. "This is my personal sanctum. Consider yourself special that I allow you in it. My office upstairs is where I conduct business, opening accounts, creating the credit cards——like the one I made for you——and it's also where the keys are created and married to their owners.

"The owners are then given a box, left alone to place whatever they deem of importance inside, and then it is locked and placed in the vault down here. What is in them, even I don't know."

"What seals them?" asked Jasmin. "Vampires can't work magic, so how do you seal them?"

"They are sealed by an ancient elven spell that is paired with the individual's key."

Jasmin turned to Elric. "I don't suppose you know anything about ancient elven magic?"

The wolf shook his head.

"That was rhetorical," she said. "Mostly."

The vampire moved to one of the bookshelves to his right and removed a brace of books. Behind them was a flat glass plate that came alive when he placed his palm against it. A green light scanned his hand, blinking as it worked to unlock a series of large, metallic bolts that allowed him to then cast open the entire bookcase, revealing a gray room beyond.

Low level lighting was activated when the door opened,

illuminating a large room that looked exactly like a bank's lock box suite. The walls were lined with miniature vaults, each with a small handle and keyhole protruding from the otherwise smooth and gleaming walls.

Arnold reached into his robe and withdrew a key of his own. He walked midway down the wall before stopping at a row of drawers. Inserting his own key, he turned the latch and swung open the tiny door. Inside rested an elaborately carved marble box, which he withdrew and placed on a table in the center of the room.

"This is the box that belonged to the fae," he said.

"Did her daughter ever come and use this box?" asked Torie.

Arnold shook his head. "No. I never saw anyone other than the older woman. She was given two-key activation. What she did with the second key, or who she gave it to, was her business."

Torie handed one of the keys to Jasmin and they both approached the box. It was adorned with tiny dragons that appeared to be part of the carving that made up the box. Two matching dragon heads protruded from each end on the front of the box. Inside the mouth was an opening for the keys.

"Okay," said Jasmin, "let's give it a shot."

The two witches placed both keys in the dragons simultaneously and turned.

Nothing happened.

"Told you, you can't open them. And neither can I," Arnold said.

Jasmin looked frustrated and placed both hands on the lid. She closed her eyes and whispered an incantation. The box flared brightly, emanating a shock of power that knocked the witch backwards a few steps.

"Ouch," said Jasmin, wringing her hands. "That elven magic is no joke."

"Maybe there is another way," said Torie. "Maybe we don't need to open it. Let me try something." She closed her eyes and held out her hands.

"Contents of this box, sealed away with a magical vow,
appear in my hands, come to me now!"

The box began to glow softly, followed by a swirl of softly glowing red smoke that escaped like steam from the locked container. It flowed slowly through the air before coalescing into the solid form of a manila envelope in Torie's hands.

"Wow," she said. "I'm surprised that worked."

"Looks like someone has mastered the art of calling to objects. Never occurred to me to try that," said Jasmin.

Torie looked at the envelope.

"Well, open it," said Fionna.

Torie hesitated, looking at Arnold. He turned away but did not leave the room as Torie broke the seal and tore it open. Inside was a small, green ledger, and inside that were pages of handwritten notes in a language Torie couldn't understand. She handed it over to Jasmin.

"It's written in fae," Jasmin said, frowning. "I can't read it. Fionna, Elric, can either of you read fae?"

Both shook their heads.

"Great," said Jasmin. "That means we have to take it back to Wednesday and hope we can trust her to translate it."

"Absolutely not," said Arnold. "It's one thing that I let you into the vault, another entirely to let you walk out of here with someone else's private property. If that were to get out, my business would be ruined overnight." He saw the look on the faces of the two witches as they deliberated over his words. "Oh for goodness sake, give it to me. I can read fae."

He took the booklet from Jasmin and glanced at the pages.

"It's a record of transactions. A checklist of…" His voice trailed off, and Torie could swear that his already pale features grew even whiter in the dim light of the vault.

"Arnold, what is it?" she asked.

The vampire swallowed hard. When he continued, his voice was soft and weak. "It's a list of the organs that…that I collected from the shifters I killed. There is also a payment log for each one."

His hands trembled as he handed the book back to Jasmin, turning his back on them.

"It's a detailed log of everything I did…between the fae woman and my old assistant Breonna."

Torie was in shock. What business did Wednesday's mother have with the hedge witch who had been controlling Arnold and driving him to attack and kill shifters.

"What the hell was your assistant involved in?" asked Jasmin.

Arnold shook his head. "I honestly have no idea. And with her dead, it's not like we can ask her."

Jasmin narrowed her eyes. "Wrong. That is exactly what we are going to do."

Chapter Eleven

"You sure about this, Jasmin?" Torie asked as they arrived back at her house and walked into the kitchen. "I mean, maybe Wednesday knows something that could help us."

"No, she doesn't know any more than she already told us," said Jasmin. "All of this is definitely starting to lead around to that mess with the shifters being killed and whoever was controlling Arnold and the hedge witch. This might be our only chance to cut the head off the hydra."

Torie started. "You don't mean that literally, do you?"

Jasmin looked at her, eyes wide. "Are you asking me if hydras exist? Of course not." She cut her eyes quickly to Elric but looked away before the werewolf could either confirm or deny the subject in question.

"Well how should I know?" asked Torie. "I didn't think werewolves and vampires existed until only a couple of months ago."

"Well, I can confidently say that we aren't facing a mythological dragon. But I am pretty sure this warlock who's in town has something to do with it."

Elric bristled. "As do I. All the more reason for the two of you to stay out of this. Turn this over to Max; let him deal with it."

"Tempting," said Jasmin, "but no. The police were no help in solving this before. Besides, if there is a warlock in town...one that feeds off witches, then it's our duty to stop him."

Torie found herself agreeing. She thought of Fionna and the unimaginable pain she had endured at losing her best friend, as well as other members of her shifter community. If someone started to suddenly hunt witches in the area, Torie didn't want to think about how she would feel. Whatever it took, she was going to help find this man and stop him.

"We still don't know for certain it's the warlock behind all this," said Torie.

"That's why we are going to ask the only person who seems to have had their grubby little fingers in this from the beginning. Breonna."

Torie felt a shiver down her spine. "I still don't like the idea of a séance."

"We don't have a choice," said Jasmin. "I mean, it may not even work. If it doesn't, then we are right back where we started; so there's no harm in trying."

Torie wanted to tell her that there was plenty of potential harm in trying. Wasn't this how the *Exorcist* had started?

"Hey, maybe we could ask my mother to help," she suggested. "Maybe she can...I don't know, find Breonna on the other side and just ask her."

Jasmin shook her head. "Death doesn't work like that. Spirits aren't just clumped together in a big elysian field, frolicking the day away. They can be wandering aimlessly for decades before they even realize they are dead; and all that time they may not have seen another non-living soul. Your mother is tethered to this house, so asking her to go out into the ether to find another spirit? You might never see her again."

Torie took a deep breath. That wasn't something she was willing to risk.

"So what do we need to do this? I don't have a Ouija board or anything like that," said Torie.

"Did you say Ouija board?" asked Fionna. She had been rummaging in the fridge and popped up at the mention of the game board. "Uh-uh, cos if that's what y'all are dragging out, I'm outta here."

"No, Fionna, we are not using a Ouija board. But you are right about one thing; you can't be here."

"What? Why not?"

"Because your emotions are far too raw. You're still angry over the passing of Taylor...and there is nothing wrong with that. But we are going to try and break through the veil between this world and that of the dead. Emotions flaring out of control, mental states that are anything less than laser focused on a single intent, are not something we can have."

Fionna placed her hands on her hips. "Yes, I am still upset over my friend being murdered. But I can control myself, you know."

"Also," continued Jasmin, "there is a chance that stray spirits may tag along with the one we summon. They may be looking for a new physical body to jump into."

"Yeah, I'm out," said Fionna, turning to head for the door. "I'm not about to become a walking spirit condom. Peace out." She held up her fist, first two fingers raised in salute to the women behind her.

Jasmin smiled and then turned to Elric.

"That goes for you too, big guy. Your energy is focused on protecting Torie…whether both of you know it or not. That could turn to fear for her during this, which will attract spirits like moths to a porch light."

Unlike Fionna, he didn't protest, but instead walked over to Torie. "Is that what you want as well?"

She ran her hands up and down his arms a few times. "Honestly, I'm going to go with Jasmin on this, because I don't know what else to do. What she is saying makes sense." She gave him a hug, breathing in his earthy scent before she pulled away.

"One more thing," said Jasmin. "You need to take Ward and Wednesday with you."

Both Elric and Torie turned to face her, mouths hanging open.

"What?" asked Jasmin. "Unless you want to explain to your ex and his pregnant fae mistress why they can't leave their rooms tonight, no matter what they hear. Besides, we still don't know what exactly is going on with that warlock. If something happens, Elric can protect them."

Torie thought about it but shook her head. "I have a better idea."

"You sure you're ready for this?" asked Jasmin.

Torie nodded. "You're right about Elric being able to protect Wednesday; and us if need be. Better to have him close by, just in case things go south. Never know when werewolf muscle might come in handy."

She was stirring a pot of green tea with a few drops of a sleeping potion she had concocted from the herbs in her workshop.

"Why not just have Jasmin put them to sleep again?" Elric asked.

"Because there is no telling how long that spell will last, for one thing," said Jasmin, "and for another, Wednesday's baby is immune to magic…it may be able to fight the spell off. But a sleeping potion will work on both Ward and Wednesday. It should keep them down and quiet until the morning. You need to stay in the guest room with them, Elric. No matter what you hear, unless we specifically call for you, do not come out of that room. Okay?"

"Very well," he replied. "I will do as you ask."

Jasmin looked at Torie and nodded. "Alright. It's time."

Torie took the tea kettle, along with two ceramic mugs, and placed them on a wooden TV tray and carried them up the staircase to the spare room her guests were sharing. She knocked lightly on the door before pushing through.

"Hi, guys," she said. "I was wondering if you'd like some tea? It's a new brew I've been working on, trying to get the taste just right. I'd love it if you'd try it and let me know what you think."

Ward was sitting at the foot of the bed, massaging Wednesday's feet as she sat propped up on a couple of pillows reading a magazine.

Ward moved to take the tray from Torie and sat it on the dresser opposite the bed.

"Torie, you didn't have to do this. We could have come down and gotten it ourselves."

"Oh, I don't mind," she said. "Plus, it's my way of saying I'm sorry for not making you feel more welcome here." She moved over to the tray and carefully filled the two mugs. "I've been toying with creating my own tea blends to maybe sell in town at one of the farmers' markets.

Plus, it will help you relax after everything you've been through the past few weeks."

"Thank you, Torie," Ward said, taking the cup from her. He turned it up, taking a big swallow. "Hmm, that's not bad at all. You might be onto something here."

She smiled, taking the second cup and offering it to Wednesday. The fae looked at her as if she had suddenly sprouted a second head.

"Yeah, I'm not drinking that," she said, wrinkling her nose. "Who knows what's in it." She narrowed her unblinking eyes at Torie.

"Babe, c'mon, we talked about this, remember?"

Torie had no idea what they had discussed, and she really didn't care. She found the mental picture of having to hold Wednesday's mouth open and pouring the potion down her throat by force rather pleasing.

Instead of brute force, however, she opted for diplomacy.

"Wednesday," she said, "it's a special herbal mixture. One that is specially formulated to help the baby. I'm betting you haven't been taking a lot of prenatal vitamins, what with all the running from the law you've been doing. This will help." She gave the fae a knowing look, stopping just short of winking at her.

Wednesday reluctantly took the cup from her.

"Well…if you're saying it's specially made for the baby, I'll try it." She turned the cup up and drank, before pausing to savor the flavor. "It's actually not bad."

Torie smiled and stepped back towards the door. "I'll leave the tray here. Just put it outside the door when you're finished, and I'll take it back downstairs later."

She closed the door behind her, then listened long enough to be certain they were still drinking the tea. Satisfied, after hearing a few more mumbled whispers, she returned to the kitchen.

"Okay, they're drinking it."

"How long until it takes effect?" asked Elric.

"It's pretty fast. They should be completely out in twenty minutes," replied Jasmin. "In the meantime, lets collect the last couple of items we need."

They went into the living room where Elric had already moved the furniture away from the center of the room and taken up the throw rug, exposing the hardwood beneath.

There was a collection of drawing pencils in various colors that Torie had found in her mother's workroom. Jasmin went about drawing a large circle in the center of the floor. They took tall, white candles and sat them at five points along the circle. Torie took notice and realized if they drew lines connecting the candles it would have drawn a pentagram.

She pointed it out to Jasmin and asked if they were going to draw a star.

"No," said Jasmin, "that's another stereotype. We don't need to draw hexagrams, pentagrams or anything else for this."

"Then why draw a circle?" asked Torie.

"Because we need to create a boundary. Something the spirit can't cross. We don't want a hedge witch breaking free of the other side and roaming around your house. For that matter, you might want to warn your mother not to make an appearance once we start this. The circle will draw in the spirit we call, but it could also attract Alva as well."

"What can I do?" asked Elric.

"Well, go into the kitchen and get some salt out of the pantry. Then, shift into your wolf form and go play babysitter." She stopped the wolf just as he turned to enter the kitchen. "Elric, I'm very serious when I say don't open that door and don't come down here no matter what you hear. If we need you, you'll know it."

He nodded, giving her a nervous smile, and walked into the kitchen.

"Jasmin, I don't think this is a good idea."

It was Alva's ghost, standing behind Jasmin, her form a hazy flicker of pale blue.

Jasmin looked from her to Torie, who only shrugged both shoulders.

"Alva…this could be our chance to figure out what is really going on here. We have to do this. And I don't want you around when it happens."

"Well, that's too bad. Cos I'm not going anywhere. I won't venture near the circle, but I'm staying put. You have no idea what could go wrong trying to summon the dead like this. It's something we were always told to never attempt."

Jasmin looked at her oldest friend. "I know. But desperate times…and all that. Besides, I've read up on this many times. How hard can it be?"

"You've never done this before?"

"No, Torie, I haven't. What do you think, I spend my Sunday evenings chatting with the spirits of my departed friends?" She glanced sheepishly at Alva. "Sorry. No offense or anything."

"None taken. It just makes me nervous what you're doing. As someone that is able to go back and forth between both sides, I'm just telling you that…well, there are things on the other side that give me the willies. If I had flesh it would be crawling the whole time I'm not on this side of the veil."

"Mom, what are you talking about? You said when you

weren't here, you weren't aware of where you were. That being on the other side felt like being asleep and here feels like being awake," said Torie.

"That's how it was. But lately, it's like I'm asleep but dreaming. Dreaming about scary things that I can't quite see…"

Torie glanced at Jasmin, not bothering to hide her concern.

"One thing at a time," Jasmin said. "Right now, we need to concentrate on summoning a dead hedge witch."

Elric entered the room and handed her a box of salt.

"Thank you, Elric. It's time now for you to go guard the guests in the house."

The wolf nodded, and in the blink of an eye shifted into his canine form, loping up the steps and out of sight.

"One last thing," Jasmin said, turning to Torie. "I need a really sharp knife."

"I can get one from the kitchen. What is it for?"

"It's for the cuts we have to make. Nothing attracts the attention of the dead like the smell of fresh blood."

Torie's face went white, which drew a smile from Jasmin. They were really about to do this. They were about to raise the dead.

Chapter Twelve

Torie walked into the kitchen, her mind numb, her legs stiff as she forced one foot in front of the other. She went to the butcher block, withdrew the sharpest knife she could find and turned just as Jasmin stepped into the room.

"We need alcohol as well," she said.

Torie blinked rapidly. nodding her head. "Oh yeah, I could definitely use a drink right now."

"What? No this isn't for us to drink, it's to sterilize the blade." She walked over to the liquor cabinet and withdrew the bottle of Carolina whiskey that sat on the center shelf.

She took the blade from Torie's hand and held it over the sink. Torie's eyes widened as she watched Jasmin pour some of the alcohol over both sides of the blade. The sight of that delicious brown liquid flowing down the sink chased whatever fear she was feeling away.

"You could have at least gotten a cup to catch that in," she grumbled." We may be about to summon the dead, but that doesn't mean we should just throw good whiskey down the drain."

102

Jasmin rolled her eyes and returned to the living room.

"So what are we going to cut?" asked Torie.

"Ourselves. Just a little slice across the palm of the hand," said Jasmin.

Torie shuddered inwardly. "Why does it have to be the hand? You said that Hollywood never got this right but that seems to be what always happens on *Supernatural* and every other vampire TV show. They're always cutting their hands, and it just looks so painful."

"Well, the cut doesn't have to be in the hand, it can be anywhere. I mean, do you want to cut your arm? Maybe your leg? You tell me where you'd like to cut."

"Honestly, I'd rather not cut anything."

"Don't worry, the cut heals very fast. It's all part of the ritual. A healing spell is layered on top of the incantation to close the wound."

Jasmin took the blade and laid it carefully on a white towel that had been draped over one of the console stands that Elric had pushed against the wall.

"And now for the salt," she said.

"Let me guess, we have to layer it on top of the circle," said Torie.

Jasmin winked at her. "Look at you catching on so fast. That's to keep the spirit trapped inside the circle. As long as the salt line remains unbroken, the spirit is trapped within."

"So all this time you mean to tell me that Dean and Sam were giving a Masters class on demonology?"

Jasmin smiled, laughing lightly as she took the salt and began to carefully trace the circle, careful to ensure that every inch of the outline was covered.

"So what happens if the hedge witch gets out of the circle?"

Jasmin completed the circle instead of looking at her

friend. "Honestly, I don't know. Like I said, I've never done this before. It's just something I've read about."

Torie looked around and could see her mother in the far corner of the room. The ghost appeared visibly disturbed, flickering in and out of view. Torie wanted to say something to her, to assure her that everything was going to be alright, that they had this under control. But in order to do that, she needed to first convince herself that everything was going to be alright.

"Okay, that's everything," said Jasmin.

"Wait, that's it? Do we need a crystal ball, some magic leaves or sage or anything like that?" asked Torie.

"All we need is our intent and our will. Never forget, that's what drives magic. Our intent."

She moved over to the console and retrieved the knife. Torie felt the hairs all along her arms stand up at the sight of the cold steel. Jasmin went and stood at the edge of the circle and motioned for Torie to follow.

She held one hand over the circle, palm up, and quickly ran the blade across her flesh, slicing deep across the surface. She squeezed her fist, causing rivulets of red to drop onto the hardwood floor inside the circle. Looking at the blade, she whispered a quick incantation, and Torie watched as the blood on the knife flared brightly and then disappeared.

"Your turn," she said, handing the hilt of the blade to her friend.

Torie took the knife in her hand and gave her friend one quick glance, biting lightly on her lower lip as she held her hand, palm up, over the circle as well. She took a deep breath and placed the sharp edge against her skin. She was quick, drawing the blade across her palm, wincing at the feel of her skin splitting open.

She quickly made a fist, squeezing her blood into the same area where Jasmin's had fallen. Walking over to the console, she placed the knife down before looking at her hand.

"Um, Jasmin, it's not closing."

"Don't worry, it will. Now come over here and stand next to me."

Torie did as she was asked and watched as Jasmin closed her eyes and began to breathe deeply; in through her nose and out through her mouth.

"Torie, light the candles."

Torie closed her eyes and pictured the candles lit as she softly said, "Ignitus."

The candles roared to life, white flames sparking and flickering into view. Torie strained her ears, realizing the house was abnormally quiet. It was as if the very walls of the structure, and any living creature within, could sense what they were doing and had retreated in fear.

"We're going to recite an incantation," said Jasmin. "From this point on, no matter what happens, do not step into the circle; and don't disturb the salt line."

Torie nodded, ignoring the lump in her throat. In her mind, she kept reciting the words Jasmin had spoken earlier; intent and will.

Those are our tools.

She followed Jasmin's lead, taking slow deep breaths in her nose and exhaling them through her mouth. She focused on her breathing and was thankful for the sense of calm that somehow made its way into her body. When she opened her eyes, Jasmin was staring at her intently. The older witch nodded, letting Torie know it was time. She took a piece of folded paper from her pocket and handed it to Torie.

Written on it was a spell. Torie looked up, nodded, and focused on reading the words in the flickering candlelight. She cursed herself for not wearing her readers, but luckily Jasmin had printed out the spell in large, legible script.

Taking a deep breath, the two witches began to cast their spell.

> *"By the charms of Anubis, I call to thee,*
> *oh shade of things I cannot see,*
> *hidden behind a veil of mist and gray,*
> *I call forth the spirit of the one I say.*
> *Breonna the witch, so dark and foul,*
> *we command you appear before us now."*

Three times they repeated the incantation, each time their voices growing more forceful, demanding the guardians that kept the dead at bay to relax their hold on the spirit world. The living room grew cold, so cold that Torie could see her breath billowing before her. The candles flared, their flames roaring to a height that reached halfway to the ceiling before suddenly falling back to their normal size. They flickered slightly in a breeze that Torie couldn't feel.

"She's here," whispered Alva from the far corner of the room.

Torie glanced at her mother, who had grown so dim and pale she was barely visible in the room.

"Where is she?" she asked.

Jasmin elbowed her lightly and pointed to an area inside the circle not far from the fireplace. At first, Torie didn't see anything. Then, she could just make out what looked like a small patch of dark fog, nearly invisible against the hardwood flooring. Had it not moved slightly, she might not have noticed it at all. It stretched out, moving the way the mist might travel across a wet knoll, before gathering itself into a ball in the center of the circle.

There it sat, pulsing in and out; like it was breathing, or mimicking its own heartbeat.

"What now?" Torie whispered, not taking her eyes off the formless mass.

"Now, we see if we can get her to talk. But remember, no matter what, don't give her any personal information. As a matter of fact, don't even answer any questions if she asks."

Jasmin took a deep breath and addressed the formless spirit.

"Is this the spirit of the now dead being that was known to us as Breonna, the hedge witch?"

Silence. But slowly the mass of fog began to unfurl itself, lengthening, appearing taller than before.

"You have to answer, spirit. Answer or be returned to the darkness from whence you came."

The blob stirred, standing a little taller. Then came a voice; low and sounding far away.

"Who are you that you call to me?"

Torie felt her skin crawl; it was like having a very sharp knife saw back and forth across a porcelain plate.

"Never mind who we are," said Jasmin, "You are bound by the rules of summation. You have to answer our questions."

A sigh rolled like a breath of fetid air across the room.

"Fine. Yes, I am Breonna. Though in life, I was far more than just a hedge witch."

Jasmin frowned, looking at Torie, wondering if she should pursue that, but then shaking her head as she turned back to the disembodied girl.

"Do you remember how you died?" asked Jasmin. "I need to make certain you aren't some trickster come to take the place of Breonna."

"Of course I remember. I was killed by the one I swore service to. I didn't live up to my part of the bargain and was outsmarted by a couple of witches and a shape-shifter."

"What was the bargain that you struck?" asked Torie, stepping forward to speak for the first time.

"To provide control of a vampire to a man, who in return would teach me magic. Who are you?"

"That's no concern of yours," said Jasmin. "You're a hedge witch. You know that men can't control magic."

"This one could. He was a very powerful warlock. And he offered to teach me things that no witch could ever know."

"Why did he want you to control a vampire?" asked Torie.

"Because the vampire was fast and strong and could get the things he needed; namely, the organs of certain shifters. You sound familiar. Can't you just tell me your name?"

"What was he planning to do with the things the vampire collected?" asked Jasmin.

"He said they were the key to the holy grail for warlocks. Where am I? I can't see…"

"You don't have to worry about where you are," said Torie. "Tell us more about this holy grail."

"I'm tired. It's draining being here. Can you see me? Do I have my body?"

"Tell us what we need to know, and maybe we'll answer that for you," said Torie. Jasmin gave her a cross look, but she ignored it. "Keep going; the holy grail."

The spirit seemed to consider this, pulsing lightly in place.

"He said there was a way to free himself from needing to be tethered to a witch for power."

"Blasphemy," said Jasmin. "And you believed him?"

"I had no reason not to. Witches were always so greedy with their magic; keeping it to themselves, looking down their noses at us hedges. Personally, I didn't care if he sucked the power out of every witch in the world and used it as he saw fit. But he said, with my help, he could break away from that. And for helping him, he would become my teacher, showing me how to use magic in ways that no witch had ever dared. Now, tell me, do I have my body?"

"No," said Torie, ignoring Jasmin's look that came her way like daggers.

"Where is it?"

"What else did the warlock tell you?" asked Jasmin. "What did he tell you about a fae woman?"

"A fae? Yes, there was a fae. I remember her now."

"What did he say?" asked Torie, stepping forward just a little.

"I feel like I'm so far away...you're fading," said the spirit. "Are you still there?"

"We're here, Breonna," said Jasmin. "Tell us about the fae."

"There is not much to tell. She was working with me to find the shifters the warlock needed. In return, she was given the one thing fae love more than anything else. But... won't you tell me your name? Otherwise, I am really tired and want to go back now." Her form began to dissolve, dropping back toward the floor in a smoky ball.

"You cannot leave until those who summoned you allow it," said Jasmin. "So you need to tell us what we need to know or we will trap your form here forever."

Something rustled in the corner behind them. Alva's

ghostly form flared brightly in response to Jasmin's threat. Instantly, Breonna's own spiritual form flared to life, glowing brightly.

"What is that?" asked Breonna. "There is another lost soul here…how is that possible?"

"Mom, calm down," said Torie, sharply.

"Mom?" echoed the spirit. "Yes, of course…I know you. I know your name!"

Breonna's form turned a blood-red hue, enlarging quickly and lurching forward. Torie yelled, moving to step back but instead she slipped and fell onto her bottom. The hedge witch leaned towards her, manifesting large glowing black eyes that bored into Torie's.

Torie screamed, kicking her legs forward as she pedaled backwards with her hands. The heel of one scrambling foot shot forward just enough to scratch through the layer of salt before them.

"No!" screamed Jasmin, throwing one arm outward to try and magically reseal the circle. She knew it was too late, and so did the vengeful spirit of the hedge witch.

The apparition grew in place, this time manifesting limbs to make itself look more humanoid. It reached past the circle, ready to throw its glowing arms around Torie.

Before she could react, Torie felt warmth brush past her; past her and through her.

Alva floated forward, throwing her blue light around the red nimbus of Breonna. She dragged the hedge witch back to the center of the circle, engulfing her in blue.

"Mom!" screamed Torie. "What are you doing? Get away from her!"

Alva's voice was calm and sure, rising above the din of the howling Breonna as the hedge witch struggled to free herself.

"Torie," said Alva, "I'm very proud of the woman you have become. Remember that." She turned her attention to Jasmin. "You know what you have to do, Jasmin. I can't hold her for long."

"Mom, no. What are you doing? Why are you doing this?"

Alva looked at her daughter. "Sometimes, you just know when you're doing the right thing."

With that, she turned and nodded at Jasmin, who raised her hands and steadied her breathing.

Closing her eyes, she clapped her hands together and said a single word.

"Askande."

And just like that, everything went quiet. The candles flared brightly once, and then the form of Alva, struggling to hold onto the hedge witch like a parent grappling a grumpy child, disappeared in a blinding flash.

Torie was shocked, looking around in disbelief. She heard Elric rushing to her side, could see his lips moving as he spoke to her, his eyes wide with concern.

"Mom! Where are you?" Torie called. "Jasmin, where is she?"

Jasmin looked at her friend, a single tear rolling down her cheek. All she could do was grasp Torie in a tight hug as the witch began to cry uncontrollably.

Chapter Thirteen

The next morning, Torie locked herself in her mother's study. It was a room she rarely visited, and one of the few she refused to move any personal belongings from. It was the one place in the house where she felt she could get to know the life her mother had created for herself in Singing Falls.

There were photographs of Alva, Jasmin, Taylor and Fionna at various points in their friendship. At the coffee shop chatting, hiking along the myriad trails that criss-crossed the town, canoeing down a lake, fishing...all of them highlighted by her mother's smile, which shone brighter than the Carolina sun.

There were other personal knick-knacks as well. Polished stones and shells that her mother had collected, displayed on shelves next to stacks of books. Her mother had been an avid reader; yet another thing that Torie didn't know.

She had missed out on so much of her mother's life. She couldn't even blame Ward for that, although she desperately wanted to. No, this was her doing. She had made the decision to cut Alva out of her life; and for what? Because it was what her husband wanted? Maybe deep down it was what she wanted as well. She told herself she had to side with her family when Ward made an ultimatum...but the truth was, she had tired of playing referee between the two of them.

What she chose was to her benefit. She turned her back on her own mother just so she didn't have to worry about fights at family get-togethers, or deflect barbs being fired from both sides. She just wanted to be left alone after so long, so she made her decision.

She had been hurt when her mother had died at the hands of Arnold, but at least knowing her spirit was still tied to the house, that they could speak whenever they wanted, had been some comfort to Torie. She had slowly been learning about her mother's life. She was able to take part in it again, as weird as that sounded.

They had been creating a second act together. Torie knew that having her mother's ghost around was a huge part of helping her to settle in to her new life in the mountains.

But now, in a single flash, that was gone. Her mother had been taken from her for a third time. Torie wasn't sure she could take it again. She felt broken and lost.

Both Jasmin and Elric had offered to stay with her, but she told them she wanted, no, she *needed*, to be alone. Even Jasmin wasn't sure what had happened to Alva's spirit. All she knew was that with the containment circle broken, Breonna would have been free in their world, and they all knew that was not something that could be allowed to happen.

Alva, being a disembodied spirit herself, had known that

better than most and did what she needed to in order to contain the hedge witch.

"You just know when you're doing the right thing," she had said.

Torie squeezed her eyes shut. No more tears came; she had cried herself dry through the night.

Now she sat in her mother's wingback reading chair, wrapped in Alva's quilt, surrounded by her mother's books on witchcraft.

There had to be something in them that would help get her mother back. There were spells and incantations for just about everything. She had begged Jasmin to perform the ritual with her again, only calling her mother back this time.

Jasmin had refused, saying it was too dangerous to do that. She had no idea if it was even possible to bring back one without the other. For all she knew, their spirits could be locked together; Alva's energy keeping Breonna from storming the gates to the land of the living. There was too much unknown about the other side, Jasmin had said. They didn't dare make the attempt again.

One thing she had been certain of, however, was that Alva wasn't gone, at least not in the sense that her spirit had been destroyed. Spirits are energy, and energy can't be created or destroyed; it just moved from one form to another, and one plane to another. When she had broken that summoning spell, she sensed that Alva was still there, just locked away somewhere that they couldn't reach.

After everyone had left, Torie had given into her despair and called out to her mother. Begging her to come back. She had even tried her own magic, reciting spell after spell as she called to Alva's spirit; all to no avail.

Finally, she had given up. Falling asleep curled in the chair, surrounded by books of magic that had failed her.

She awoke to voices chatting happily in her kitchen.

The stress of the previous night, coupled with only an hour of sleep, played with her mind, and for a second she couldn't remember who would be in her house.

She stumbled into the kitchen to find Wednesday making coffee and Ward sitting at the island looking at an old magazine he had found.

"Well hey, Torie. You were right. That tea was amazing; I slept like the dead," Ward said.

Wednesday turned to face Torie, arching an eyebrow. "Speaking of the dead...what happened down here. It smells like something...very deep went down." She leveled a look at Torie.

Ward looked confused. "I don't smell anything."

"Pregnancy nose, honey," Wednesday said. "You know my senses have been getting sharper lately." She never took her eyes off Torie.

"Jasmin and Fionna stayed a little later than I anticipated," said Torie, "We had an impromptu girls' night."

"Oh? Did you guys raise a little hell?" asked Wednesday.

"As a matter of fact, we did. Maybe I'll tell you about it sometime. I'm going to go lie down." She turned her back and walked towards her bedroom, only to be stopped by Ward's voice.

"Um, that weird looking dog of yours is hanging around out back."

Torie looked outside and saw Elric pacing back and forth on the back patio. She went through the workroom and pushed open the door. Immediately he trotted past her, through the kitchen, and headed for the bedroom.

"Gross," said Wednesday. "Dogs like that belong outside."

"Careful," said Torie, walking past them, "unlike some, I invited him into my house."

She ignored the scorned look Wednesday gave her and followed Elric into her bedroom. She sank onto the floor beside him and buried her face into his fur and cried anew.

She cried until she was spent, and then slowly sank into a slumber. She was barely aware of being scooped up in two strong, warm arms and laid gently in her bed. The covers were carefully drawn up around her, and she sank into a deep, dreamless sleep.

She awoke to the fading light of day as the warm, evening light washed her room with tendrils of orange and yellow bands. She stretched, her back and hips cramped. It had been one of those sleeps where she had been so exhausted, she didn't turn over or stretch while she was out. It was times like this she really felt her age. When did her bones start to creak? And when did she start making that groaning noise when she had to lift herself off her pillow?

She swung her legs over the edge of the bed, and that was when she noticed she was still wearing her clothing from the night before. She stood, arching her back to chase away the stiffness and made her way over to her dresser to inspect herself in the mirror.

She looked as she felt. Bags under her eyes, hair akimbo and the make-up she had been wearing was now wearing her. She cocked her head to one side, listening for the unwanted voices of the two people she was beginning to think of as emotional squatters. Luckily, she didn't hear anything but blessed quiet in the house.

"*They're with Jasmin and Fionna,*" said Elric, directly into her mind.

His voice startled her, and she spun around, shocked to

see the large wolf curled in a ball on the floor, near the bedroom door.

"Elric," she said aloud, "I didn't know you were still here." She blushed, remembering the harpy who had just been peering back at her from the mirror. She turned away from him just as he shifted into human form and walked up beside her. "I'm a mess. You shouldn't look at me like this."

He wrapped his arms around her and spun her around to face him. He held her close, resting his chin on the top of her head.

"Are you hungry?" he asked. "Or thirsty? I can make you some coffee."

She smiled. "No. I should eat something, but right now, I just don't have the desire." She pulled back from him just enough to peer up into his eyes. "And what do you mean my house guests are with Fionna and Jasmin?"

"Well, when I came in this morning, I could sense the way they disturbed you. Your nerves were raw. So after I put you to bed, I snuck back out and called Jasmin. I told her you really needed some uninterrupted rest. She agreed and came over. She convinced them to go with her to Fionna's house, explaining that Glen was a nurse anesthetist and that it was probably a good idea to have her look over Wednesday. Just to make sure everything was as it should be with the baby."

"And Wednesday agreed to that?" asked Torie, skeptically.

"Jasmin can be very persuasive."

Torie laughed. Seeing that would have almost been worth losing a little of the sleep she so obviously needed.

"Fionna agreed to make dinner to keep them there for a while as well. Apparently, Wednesday thinks you tried to poison her, and she is determined to convince Ward of that."

"Let her. Maybe they would feel safer in one of the town bed and breakfasts," Torie mumbled. She shook her head, returning to the bed to sit on the edge. "I'm sorry. I'm just…I feel so tired and wasted. I just want to find out what is going on, who killed Wednesday's mother, let her have her baby, and then kick them all to the curb to fend for themselves." Again she laughed, throwing herself backwards on the bed.

Elric laid beside her, the two of them gazing up at the ceiling. He looked over at her and smiled.

"Ugh, I must look a fright to you."

"Not at all. You look beautiful."

"I wish we could go away together. Just the two of us. Maybe when this is over?"

"I'd like that. We could go camping. Or even better, out to the coast. I've never seen the ocean."

Torie propped herself up on one elbow, staring into his eyes. "Never? Well then, that's something we definitely have to correct. I almost feel jealous…that you get to see something so magical and beautiful for the first time."

"As corny as it sounds, I feel that every time I look at you."

Torie blushed and swiped at him playfully. "Stop it, flirt."

"And the thought of seeing the ocean, experiencing it with all my senses; smelling the salt air, feeling the spray of waves, hearing the crash of water breaking over rocks…all things I've heard about but never seen. It's something I've always wanted to do."

"Wow. When you put it like that, I'm really jealous."

He propped himself up as well, reaching over to play

with a stray strand of her hair that fell over her shoulder. "I wish I could show you the world through my eyes."

Torie sat up, her mind racing.

"Maybe you could," she said. "Do you trust me?"

"Always," he replied, sitting up and watching her closely.

She turned to face him and placed both of her hands lightly on the sides of his head. She leaned forward, until both of their foreheads were touching. She closed her eyes and began to speak.

"I wish I may, I wish I might,
see through the eyes of this wolf tonight."

Then her body crumpled back onto the bed. Her eyes were closed, and her breath was shallow but steady.

"Torie!" screamed Elric, feeling a flush of panic rise in his throat.

"Elric, it's okay. I'm fine. I'm right here…with you."

Her words were crystal clear in his mind, even more so than usual. If he were being honest, it was almost as if he had thought it himself.

"Close your eyes," she said. "Feel me."

He did as she asked, and almost immediately he recognized her touch inside his mind. It wasn't like before when they communicated telepathically. He knew that part of her, the consciousness that lived within her, was now living within him. He could feel her marveling at the sensation as well.

He stood up slowly.

"Whoa," Torie said. "I just got a rush of vertigo. I'm not used to seeing everything from a foot taller. That might take some getting used to."

Elric felt the urge to flex, bending his arm until his biceps strained at the fabric of his tee shirt.

"So strong. So much power," Torie said.

"This…is weird," Elric said.

"You said you wished I could see the world through your eyes. Well, now I can. Show me everything."

Elric smiled and laughed out loud.

"Fine," he said. "Hold on tight."

With that, he leapt into the air, shifting to a wolf in mid-air, and landed on the run. Sprinting out of the bedroom and through the kitchen, he leapt high enough to clear the island and vaulted through the half-open patio doors.

Once outside, he increased his speed to a dizzying degree and raced through the meadow at the back of Torie's house and into the woods.

He trusted his nose to inhale the scents around him, sorting and filing them away as he followed a vapor trail that was invisible to the naked eye, but to him it might as well have been a path lit by neon-colored rope lights. Around him, the forest came alive in a way that Torie could never have imagined. Every sound, no matter how small or dim, entered his twitching ears and was mapped to a scent that resided in his memory.

Everything had a place and was immediately familiar to Elric. These were his woods, and he knew them intimately.

He bounded effortlessly over rock and fallen trees. The pads on the bottom of his paws sent out vibrations that echoed off the surrounding woods and bounced back to him, acting as yet another form of guidance to him.

Torie was awash in senses; she saw, heard, smelled, felt and even tasted everything all at once.

In no time they were miles from her house, deep in the mountains in an area she was not familiar with. She tapped into Elric's mind and knew this was a special place to him. There were no humans here. This was an unspoiled area of the forest that made him feel instantly happy.

They came to a creek, and Elric stopped long enough to take a cool drink from the running water. To Torie, it was the best water she had ever tasted; so cold that it burned going down the wolf's throat.

Elric looked up only to see a large black bear, crouched not ten feet from them, also drinking from the water. The bear looked at them, huffed slightly, before turning and lumbering back into the woods.

Torie was amazed at the utter lack of fear she felt. She wasn't anxious or worried. She felt at peace. She might have been sharing another's body, but at that moment, they felt like a single person.

Then, as if some higher power decided that there was indeed too much of a good thing; she felt it.

Or rather Elric did. Someone, no *something*, had made its way into his world. He lifted his nose and sniffed deeply.

An acrid scent entered his brain; a smell that had no corresponding memory with which to map it.

Too late, he recognized the smell of danger and death, but before he could run, a blast of magic, dark and crackling, struck him in the side.

He howled, and Torie screamed in the back of his mind as they were sent tumbling across the stream and into the muddy embankment on the other side.

Chapter Fourteen

Jasmin sat in the large, well-appointed sitting room of the house owned by Fionna and Glen. The house was a large English Tudor that almost looked out of place perched on the mountainside overlooking a steep ravine. The front of the house was all stone and wood, high peaked roof, with a towering stone arch you had to pass under in order to reach the imposing double glass door.

Inside, the house had been painted a soothing earth tone, with impressive wainscoting that ran throughout. The double story entryway opened to a large formal living room to one side and an office with French doors to another.

Jasmin sat in the living room, trying not to lose her mind as Ward droned on and on about how rough his life had been since going on the run.

Finally, she'd had enough. "You know I'm not going to feel the least bit sorry for you, right?" He looked at her, his eyes almost comically large. "I mean, you're a fugitive from the law. You did horrible things that ruined peoples lives. You're a terrible human being, and I don't feel sorry for you. You have to know the shit show that is your life is because of the things you did."

Ward sat back, putting down the glass of water he had been sipping.

"It's not always so cut and dry," he said. "I'm sure Torie told you all about me, but you don't know what our relationship was like. You don't know me."

"I don't care to know you, Ward. Your actions speak volumes about the kind of man you are."

He didn't say anything, opting to fold his arms across his chest and sink back into the love seat he was resting on.

Thankfully, the awkward silence was broken by the light chatter and laughter as Wednesday walked back into the room, escorted by Fionna and Glen.

"How is she?" Ward asked, standing to greet them.

"She's fine," said Glen. "She's as healthy as anyone I've ever seen. I'm not a doctor, but just from a basic physical standpoint, she is the picture of health. The baby's heartbeat is strong and regular. Judging from the way she is carrying, I'd say she's really only days away from giving birth. You know, you really should be ready to get her to a hospital."

Fionna looked from Wednesday to Jasmin before turning to her wife.

"We talked about that," said Fionna. "You know they can't go to a hospital." She gave Glen a knowing look.

Glen nodded, her lips pursed tightly. "Well, just so you know, I'm not a doctor, and I certainly am not qualified to oversee the birth of...one of your special friends."

Jasmin stepped in, smiling. "We are so thankful for all you've done for us now and in the past, Glen. We would never dream of putting you in any situation that makes you uncomfortable."

123

"Uh-huh. Right," replied Glen, her tone drier than the Sahara.

"I'm serious. I don't know if I officially thanked you for all you did during that nastiness with Arnold. You saved Eddie. So thank you."

Glen blushed, nodding her head. "I'm a nurse. It's what we do."

"But," said Jasmin slyly, "I do need to talk to Wednesday about things that Ward doesn't need to hear. Could you maybe…?"

Glen rolled her eyes good naturedly and turned to face Ward.

"Hey, do you know anything about old cars?" she asked.

"Um, yeah, cars are one of my passions," he replied, his ears perking up.

"Well, I've got this old '67 Mustang Fastback in the shed that I want to restore. But for the life of me, I just don't know where to start. Or even if it's worth trying to restore. I'd love to bounce some ideas off you if you have a minute."

He was up and starting for the door almost before she had finished her sentence. Then he turned to Wednesday mid-stride.

"Honey, is it okay if I take a look? Just for a sec?"

Wednesday smiled in response, waving her hand lightly at him. "Go. Have fun."

As soon as they were out the door, Fionna turned to Jasmin.

"What is she talking about? I can guarantee she knows more about cars than he does. She can take that thing apart and put it back together blindfolded if she had to."

"It's obviously a ruse," said Wednesday. "She was getting him out of here so your friend here can grill me about whatever it is she and Torie were doing last night back at the house."

Fionna stared at her, then looked over to Jasmin. "Did you tell her about that?"

"Didn't have to," Wednesday said, answering for Jasmin. "The place reeked of high magic this morning. You guys did something very big and very naughty I'm thinking."

Jasmin rolled her eyes, not bothering to hide her annoyance or dislike of the fae.

"We held a summoning. We raised the spirit of Arnold's dead assistant. We needed to find out what she knew about what is going on around here."

This caught Wednesday's attention, and she leaned forward, every inch of her attuned to what Jasmin was saying.

"You two actually called forth a spirit?" she asked, whistling in admiration. "That's big-girl magic. You're better than I thought."

"What did you find out?" asked Fionna.

"That she was working with your mother," Jasmin said, nodding in Wednesday's direction, "to help Arnold gather the organs of the slaughtered shifters. She was collecting payment for them."

"You lie!" said Wednesday, her body stiffening as her face contorted into a mask of rage. "How dare you say something like that."

Jasmin paused. Wednesday's reaction was real; not forced or rehearsed. She didn't know what her mother was up to.

"I wish I was lying. But it's true. So, time for you to come clean. If you know something, speak up. What was your mother into? What do you really know about the warlock who fathered your child?"

"I've told you what I know about him," she said, her voice shaking with anger. "He looked like Ward. I figured I could pass the kid off with Ward, and if the child had magical abilities, then that would be a plus."

Jasmin paced the floor. "It doesn't make sense. It can't just be a coincidence that your mother is tied to him through a hedge witch who was controlling Arnold. And now you show up pregnant by the same warlock that is central to all of this?"

"I don't know what you want me to say," said Wednesday. "My mother and I hadn't spoken in a while. I left Singing Falls because I wanted more than to just be cooped up in her bunker house. That life wasn't for me. I didn't want to be just any fae."

"Wait," said Jasmin. "When your mother approached us to find you, she said that you had recently cut off communication with her unexpectedly. That she was worried something had happened to you."

"Yeah," said Fionna. "She even said you had been seeing someone just before you disappeared."

Wednesday frowned. "That's not true. We hadn't been talking. She also didn't know I was seeing Ward. She would have never approved of me getting involved with a human male."

"Then she lied," said Jasmin. "Question is, why? Why would she want us to find you?"

"Jasmin, what else did the spirit say?" asked Wednesday.

"She said the warlock was working on something big. Something that he called the holy grail for warlocks. And in exchange he was giving your mother something that all fae craved more than anything else. Do you know what that could be?"

Wednesday didn't say anything, but something changed in her countenance.

"Oh, she knows something," said Fionna, moving towards the fae. She cracked her knuckles. "Do you want me to make her talk?"

"Fionna, stop," said Jasmin. "What did I tell you about re-watching *The Sopranos*? This is not how we do things."

"You said she's immune to magic," said Fionna, eying the fae. "But I'm betting a good old, fresh can of whoop ass can get through to her."

"Girl, she is pregnant," said Jasmin. "And ain't nobody buying your tough-guy act. You are not about to hurt this woman."

She hoped she was right. The old Fionna wouldn't have hurt a fly. But after Taylor's death, this Fionna was different. She was quick to anger and not as easy to calm down when she was upset. Fionna made a mental note to deal with that after they had worked through everything else.

Wednesday shifted on the couch, settling back.

"That sounds familiar," she said. "The part about the holy grail. Not the part about what every fae wants."

"Well, go ahead," said Jasmin. "Tell us what you know."

She looked a little hesitant before continuing. "It was… pillow talk. After we finished, before he drifted off to sleep and I sneaked out. I asked him what he was doing in town. He said he was looking for his holy grail and had been close to finding it. He mentioned that he had thought it was lost but had recently found it again. I don't know what he meant by that, honestly. And I hadn't thought about it until you mentioned it just now."

"You said you knew he possessed magic," said Jasmin. "Was it active that night? Meaning, was he using it?"

"Oh, he used it alright. Over, and over, and over

again…" she said, closing her eyes as memories washed over her body.

"Gross," said Fionna.

"So you do know how magic for warlocks works, right?" asked Jasmin.

"Sure," said Wednesday. "He has to have a source."

"So it never bothered you that he probably just drained some witch in order to provide you with a night of carnal delight?" asked Jasmin.

"Carnal delight? Jeez, just how old are you?" asked Wednesday. "And yes, I knew what he had probably done. But it didn't matter at the time. Besides, who said it was a witch?"

"We act as batteries for warlocks," said Jasmin.

"True. But so can any supernatural with enough juice in them."

Jasmin blinked, a million thoughts running through her mind.

"Wait, you didn't know that? Witches might be best, but they aren't the only ones. Plus, it depends on the warlock. I've heard of some that have a taste for elves only, or even the mystical energy given off by vampires."

"Or a fae?" said Jasmin.

Wednesday thought for a moment. "Yes, I never thought of that, but I'm sure we are no different."

"Wednesday, do you have any active magical abilities?" asked Jasmin.

She shook her head. "No. That particular gift skipped me. My mother did, but not me."

"What do you mean it skipped you?"

"With fae, magic can often skip a generation."

Something in the back of Jasmin's mind was starting to

stir. There was a thread there, one that she began to mentally pick at.

Her thoughts were interrupted by a large crash that came from the front door. The sound of wood splintering and glass shattering filled the living room.

"What the hell?" cried Fionna, heading for the entryway. She gasped when she reached the foyer, staring at the floor before her.

Jasmin and Wednesday were at her side instantly, each shocked to see Elric, his wolf form bloodied and cut, lying atop the front door he had just crashed through. His breathing was clipped and shallow, and a low, weak growl was all that emanated from his chest.

Before anyone could move, Glen and Ward came running up to the door.

"Oh my God," said Ward. "Is that Torie's dog? What happened to him?"

"Elric," said Jasmin, bending over to reach for the wounded creature. She jumped back instantly, almost as if she had been scorched by fire.

"What's wrong?" asked Fionna. "What is it?"

Jasmin's hand flew to her mouth, her eyes wide.

"Torie," she said. "That's Torie."

"What? What are you talking about?" quizzed Ward. "That's clearly…"

Before he could finish the sentence, the wolf began to change. Its form elongated, the hair dropping away, the limbs lengthening and becoming more human. In a matter of seconds, the beast became a man; bruised and cut, bleeding out on the floor.

Ward stared in disbelief, then his eyes rolled into the back of his head, and he dropped to the floor in a heap.

"Well," said Wednesday. "Looks like the cat, or rather the dog, is out of the bag."

Chapter Fifteen

"Holy Mother of God!" exclaimed Glen. "Is this what our lives have become, Fionna? Half-dead shifters just dropping out of the sky on us?"

Fionna didn't respond, dropping instead beside her fallen friend.

"Glen, get your bag!" said Jasmin, kneeling beside Fionna.

"Jas, what do you mean this is Torie?" asked Fionna.

"I don't know how to explain it, other than to say that this is Elric…but it's Torie too."

"What could do that to a werewolf?" asked Wednesday. She had taken a few steps back from the body, one hand instinctively covering her stomach.

Jasmin closed her eyes and placed both hands on Elric's body. She whispered an incantation as her hands moved across his form.

"Magic," she said. "Black magic from the feel of it. Fionna, can you hear him?"

Fionna shifted to her squirrel form just as Glen came

racing back into the room, carrying what looked like a red and white tackle box. She flipped it open to reveal a fully stocked medical carrier with multiple trays of vials and syringes. She quickly flipped open a vial of clear liquid and began drawing a syringe full of the fluid.

Fionna shifted back to human, her eyes wide. "He's unconscious. I can't reach him. All I'm getting are images of pain and…fear."

"Wolves aren't afraid of anything," said Wednesday.

"That's probably Torie in there you're feeling," said Jasmin. "We need to get her out, but…I don't know how."

They watched as Elric's body began to stiffen, accompanied by the sound of bones grinding.

"Christ, he's healing," said Glen, jabbing the needle she held into his arm and depressing the stopper on the syringe.

"Don't put him any further under than he already is," said Jasmin. "We have no idea what happened to them."

"I'm just giving him a shot of adrenaline," said Glen. "He's close to shock; his breathing is irregular as well. This will help jolt him enough. Maybe help to jump start his healing." She ran her hands over his body, probing the black bruises deeply, feeling the bones shift under her touch.

They watched as the gashes in his sides slowly began to close, the flow of blood slowing as the flesh began to knit itself back together.

A moan behind them caused them all to jump. In the frenzy, they had forgotten all about Ward.

"Keep doing whatever you're doing," said Wednesday. "I'll take care of him." She moved to his side, stooping down to hold his head as he slowly began to recover consciousness.

Jasmin turned back to Elric and placed both hands on

his head, helping to steady it as his body put itself back together.

She closed her eyes, and when she opened them, they had turned a milky white.

"He's healing his physical body," she said. "I'm going to see if I can flush out any remnants of dark magic."

It was a strain; even for a practitioner as skilled as Jasmin. The blackness was like a living tar, trying to work its way into the werewolf. Her hands hovered above his form and she began to move them over his body, focusing on the darkness that was festering within.

She pulled at it, commanding it to release its hold. Every time she lost her grip on it, she could feel something helping her. Something was pushing it out of the shifter.

Something or someone.

She could sense Torie's hand, helping to expel the evil that was trying to bond to the werewolf. Elric's body heaved, his back arching wildly under her power. Together, the two witches were able to cast the darkness out.

Fionna and Glen watched in amazement as dark energy swirled above the werewolf, creeping out of his very pores into the air above him. Jasmin gathered it, containing it in a ball of swirling yellow light.

"Stand back," she said, standing.

Lifting both hands over her head, she brought the dark matter into the air. With a heave of power, she sent the ball through the smashed door and out of the house. There, the ball exploded in a bright display of light, taking the dark magic with it.

Jasmin dropped to her knees, totally drained of energy. Fionna rushed to her side, helping to steady the witch.

"What was that?" asked Ward, sitting up next to Wednesday. He had been watching the display, his mouth agape. "What is happening here? And who, or what, is that?"

He pointed at Elric, whose breathing was returning to normal now, his naked form was covered in a blanket of sweat.

"Honey, we have a lot to talk about," said Wednesday, "and I promise I'll tell you everything in just a bit. But for right now, let's just keep quiet."

"Is…is he awake?" asked Jasmin.

Glen moved to Elric's head and lifted his eyelids, shining a small penlight into them.

"He's coming around," she said.

The werewolf groaned, reaching for his head.

"Easy there," said Fionna, helping to support his head. "Take it easy for a minute. Can someone get him a glass of water?"

Glen ran from the room, returning with a large glass. She held his hand as he sipped gingerly.

"Thank you," he said, his voice hoarse and gravelly.

"Elric, what happened to you?" asked Fionna. She brought a blanket to him that had been slung across the back of one of the sitting room couches.

"Thank you," he managed, covering his nakedness. "I… I'm not sure. One minute we were in the woods. The next…" His voice trailed off as he squinted his eyes, trying to piece his memory back together.

"Where is Torie?" Jasmin asked, making her way to her feet. She was still groggy from the expenditure of energy, but she had to know what had happened to her friend.

"Torie!" said Elric, his eyes wide with fear. Then, sensing something that the others could not, he closed his eyes and struggled to calm his breathing. "She's okay. She's here with me."

Jasmin inhaled slowly, trying to contain her feelings.

"Can I speak with her…or, I don't know, can she hear me?"

"Yes, I can hear you. Are you okay, Jasmin?" came the reply. It was still Elric's deep voice, but the cadence belonged to Torie. The effect was unnerving, to say the least.

Jasmin exhaled audibly and nodded.

"Girl, what are you doing? How are you doing this?" Jasmin questioned.

"I performed a little spell. One that let me be part of Elric, to see through his eyes."

"What happened to you? Elric's memory is spotty. Do you know?"

"I think so…we were running through the woods, racing to a point in the forest where we were totally alone. Only we weren't alone. There was a presence there…but I didn't sense it until it was too late. We were drinking from a creek, and suddenly someone attacked us with magic.

"Elric went into fight or flight mode. I could feel his human side slip away. He became all wolf, seeking to protect me. His instincts took over, and I couldn't reach him anymore. I could only watch, like I was outside of my body looking at everything from a third person's perspective."

"What did you see?" asked Jasmin.

"A man, the warlock I presume, on a knoll behind us. He had wrapped himself in magic to cloak his presence. He attacked from behind, hurling black light at us. We had been thrown across the water, and he continued to attack. He was so fast…faster than a human should be able to move. He lunged across the creek, attacking us again. He had a staff that he used to wield wild magic. He tried to club us, smashing at Elric's head with the end of his staff.

"But as fast as he was, Elric was faster. He dodged the blows, leaping from side to side while trying to fight back. He nearly got him a couple of times. His teeth came close to snapping the man's arm. But each time he would manage to evade the bite, and he would swing his staff, sending bolt after bolt of magic at Elric.

"A couple of times, he was able to slip past Elric's guard and land some blows on his side. The pain was indescribable. I could hear bones crunching with the hits. It was terrible. I thought we were going to die.

"Then, he started to chant, Jasmin; in a language I couldn't understand. But I could feel the effect of the words. It was a spell; one that was trying to suck the very life out of us. I could feel it, like a thousand little leeches feeding off us.

"That was when I really panicked. Part of me screamed as hard as I could, and I reached out with my own magic. Somehow, Elric channeled it and a blast of blue light struck out, leveling the man and a good part of the woods we were in.

"We turned and ran, not bothering to see if the warlock was still alive or anything. I remember having a mental picture of you and Fionna in my mind as I started to black out. All I could think was that I was so sorry for letting you guys down. The next thing I know, we were waking up here, just a few minutes ago."

Elric shook his head, his eyes refocusing on Jasmin.

"I don't remember that. I just remember thinking I had to fight. And then I saw you in my mind's eye and knew I had to get to you. That's really it."

Jasmin didn't say anything but started to pace the floor. She was mumbling to herself and shaking her head.

"Jasmin, what is it?" asked Fionna.

Jasmin wheeled, facing Torie.

"What were you thinking, Torie? Using your magic through Elric like that could have killed him. And just merging yourself into him like this…it's reckless!"

Torie didn't say anything but Elric dropped his head in shame.

"Is someone going to tell me what is going on?" asked Ward.

"Welcome to my wacky hometown," said Wednesday. "Where most of the citizens are not what they appear." She looked at Jasmin and raised an eyebrow.

"Fine," said Jasmin. "I'm a witch, so is Torie. Fionna is a squirrel shifter. You've met Elric in both of his forms. He's a werewolf."

Ward took in the scene in silence. Then he turned to his mistress.

"Is this some kind of joke? Something you cooked up with your friends here to haze the new guy in town?"

She shook her head. "They aren't my friends, Ward. But they are telling you the truth. You saw Elric turn with your own eyes."

"I…I'm not sure what I saw." He turned his eyes to Wednesday. "And if it were true…what about you?"

She took a deep breath. "I'm a fae. Some call us fairy folk. But yeah, I'm part of the supernatural community here. That's why I wanted us to come back here and stay with my mother for a while. The feds can't track us here. This whole town is steeped in magic."

He swallowed hard, and they could see the wheels spinning in his mind. He nodded, accepting one statement was causing more questions to race through his mind.

"And the baby?" he asked.

Wednesday tensed. "The baby is a mix of human and fae. But will be magical; I can feel that."

Jasmin and Fionna exchanged glances with the fae. Wednesday's face seemed to be pleading with them. Jasmin shrugged and turned back to Elric.

"Are you up to traveling? We need to get out of here, and I need your senses to make sure the warlock isn't tracking you."

Elric nodded. "Yeah, I'm already feeling better."

Jasmin turned to leave the room but quickly turned to face him. "Elric, where is Torie's body?"

"In her bed," he said. "Why?"

Jasmin's eyes grew wide. "Torie, you left your body unprotected? With a warlock that feeds off magical energies hunting in the area?"

Fear flooded Elric's features. "You guys get there as quickly as you can. I'm taking the short cut."

Though shifting caused him more pain, he transformed into his wolf form and left the house, speeding down the mountainside.

Chapter Sixteen

The sight of her own body lying perfectly still on her bed was a sight Torie had not prepared herself for.

Is that what I'll look like when I'm dead?

Why would you think such a thing? replied Elric. *No one is dying anytime soon.*

They were both thankful nothing had happened. What that something could have been, Torie didn't want to think about. The panic in Jasmin's voice when she asked where her body was had freaked Torie out.

That fear had given speed to Elric. Even though he needed the rest, he had made it back to her house in record time. The back door was still open, and Torie found herself cursing at her stupidity. The relief that flooded them both was overwhelming when they entered the bedroom to find her undisturbed.

Elric shifted back to human form and stared down at the resting form.

"What do you need me to do?" he asked.

Nothing. Just close your eyes and try to settle your thoughts.
Then, he opened his mouth and spoke.

"May the powers that be,
return me to me."

A ripple of energy passed over the werewolf's body as energy shimmered, passing from him to Torie's form.

She sat up, stretching and arching her back. It was definitely good to be back in her own form, although she realized she would definitely miss the strength of a wolf's frame.

"Are you okay?" Elric asked, reaching for her.

"Actually, I feel pretty good," said Torie. It was true. She realized a lot of the little aches and pains she had become used to over the last couple of years weren't bothering her as much. "But how are you?"

She took a long look at the wolf. The cuts on his body were healing, but the bruises looked especially mean; black, blue and yellow. He legitimately looked like he had been hit by a truck.

"Draw a hot bath, I'm going to the kitchen to get you some Epsom salts and a healing potion. I want you to soak in that for a while."

He didn't argue and went to the bath to run some water as she hurried for the kitchen. Gathering the needed items, she returned to the bathroom just as the tub was nearly filled. She added the salts, followed by a couple of vials of another greenish liquid which caused the water to sparkle brilliantly.

"This will help settle the bruising and help return your energy," she said as he eased his body into the welcoming warmth.

"Torie, thank you. And I hope I didn't get you into any trouble. Jasmin seemed pretty pissed at what we did."

She smiled. "You didn't do anything I didn't want to do. And don't worry, I can handle Jasmin."

I hope, she thought as she left the room.

"I heard that," Elric called after her as she eased the bathroom door shut.

She returned to the kitchen and took out a pad and pencil, and quickly started writing on it. The front door opened without a knock and Jasmin rushed in, followed by Fionna, Ward and Wednesday.

Jasmin took a look at Torie and frowned.

"Is that you?" she asked.

"You know it is," replied Torie.

Fionna ran up to her and hugged her. "Torie, are you alright? When I saw the shape Elric was in, I was terrified for you."

"Thanks, Fionna, but I'm good. Really."

Fionna leaned in as she hugged her and whispered in her ear. "Wednesday pretty much told Ward everything, but she didn't tell him the baby wasn't his. I was going to mention it, but decided I'm not going to be catty like that. Besides, I thought it might be more fun if you told him." She smiled and released her friend, stepping back.

"Nope. Not my business. I'm not gonna be messy like that," said Torie.

"Have you swept the place for any signs of disturbance since you came back? Was anyone in here?" asked Jasmin.

Torie hadn't thought of that. Thinking that someone might have been in the house, looking at her body, sent chills up her spine.

"Nothing seemed to have been disturbed," said Torie.

"But no, I didn't do anything more than a cursory evaluation once we got back."

Jasmin frowned. "Ward, why don't you take Wednesday upstairs and relax a bit. She's been through a lot, and so have you, what with all you've just learned."

"Yeah, I'd like to lie down a bit," he said, sensing that Jasmin wasn't really asking him if he'd like to leave the room.

Once they were gone, she turned to Torie.

"What were you thinking? Do you know what could have happened?"

Torie stammered in her defense. "Honestly, I just wanted to feel strong. To literally see the world as a wolf does. I guess I just didn't think."

"No, you didn't," said Jasmin, cutting her off. "What if you had gotten stuck inside him? What if that warlock had killed him? Where would you be then? What if it was too much for his werewolf instincts and his humanity had been shut down? He can't speak in wolf form, so that means you wouldn't have been able to utter any incantations…even if you wanted to."

She turned, her hand on her head, pacing the length of the kitchen island.

"Torie, we raised the spirit of a dead hedge witch in this house last night. We swept aside the veil to let her in. What if something else had come across with her and was in here and just happened to notice the body of a very powerful witch lying around, soulless? Do you know what could have happened?" She grabbed her friend and hugged her tight. "I…I don't want to lose you too. Promise me you will never do something like that again."

Fionna ran over to the two of them and threw her arms around them both, sobbing into their shoulders.

"Nothing bad happened, you guys," she said, "but I'm with Jasmin; if something had happened to you, I don't know what I would have done. Other than Glen, you two are my family. The family I choose. So from now on, we all promise to not take stupid chances. Agreed?"

Torie nodded, not trusting her voice.

"I promise," she finally managed to squeak out as they broke their embrace.

Fionna was wiping her eyes. "But, since you did do it... what was it like?"

Torie laughed weakly. "Transcendent. I can't describe how it felt, but Jasmin is right. It was foolish."

"Torie, do you remember anything else about the warlock who attacked you?" Jasmin asked.

She shook her head but reached for the paper she had been writing on.

"I was making notes. Even now, everything about him is starting to fade from memory. I wanted to write down everything before it faded."

"Smart move," said Jasmin. "I learned a couple of things from Wednesday as well." She repeated everything she and the fae had discussed while at Fionna's house. "So that explains why you were attacked," she added.

"He was after magic?" asked Torie.

Jasmin nodded. "It would make sense. If he can use the mystical energies of any supernatural, then you being fused with a werewolf would have stood out like a nuke to him. He was drawn to you. You were lucky to get away."

"Do you still think he'll be looking for them?" asked Fionna.

"Most definitely. The black magic I pulled out of Elric was trying to attach itself to him like a tick. I'm betting once the warlock got a taste of that, he'll want more."

"So what do we do?" asked Torie.

"I'm thinking about that," said Jasmin. "I still think there is a critical piece of the puzzle we are missing, and it has to do with that fae upstairs. All of this comes back to her, or more superficially, her mother. If the warlock was behind Arnold's attacks, and she was working with him from the beginning, then that's where our answer lies."

"Do you believe Wednesday when she said she doesn't have anything to do with it?" questioned Torie.

"I believe that she isn't knowingly involved."

"Why isn't she upset?" Fionna asked out of the blue.

"What do you mean?"

"Well, she just finds out that her mother is dead, and she really hasn't shown any emotion over it. You were a mess when your mother passed away. I was destroyed over Taylor. But she's almost like business as usual."

"Business as usual," said Jasmin, thinking over the phrase. "That ledger in the lock box at Arnold's, it detailed payment, right?"

"Yes," said Torie. "Next to each entry, there was a dollar amount."

"But they were all made out to Wednesday's mother," said Jasmin. "There were none made out to Breonna, and she was the one controlling Arnold."

"True," said Torie. "But she said she was getting paid in knowledge."

"That's right," said Jasmin. "He was going to teach her real magic. But in order to do that he had to break free of only being able to siphon off other magical creatures. Maybe that's the missing piece."

"I don't follow," said Torie.

"Maybe that's what he needed the shifter organs for. Maybe he was creating some spell, or potion that would eliminate his need for an external power source. Some of the shifters he collected were very strong; that's why he needed Arnold. A vampire could overpower most shifters."

"And to control Arnold, he used Breonna. A hedge witch that he could manipulate."

"Why wouldn't he just use his own power to control Arnold?" asked Fionna. "Cut out the middle man."

"Because he couldn't. At least not yet. He wouldn't have risked Arnold breaking free of his spell if he ever ran out of energy," said Jasmin.

"And he couldn't use Breonna as his power source because hedge witches don't generate magic, they deal mostly in potions and powders," added Torie. "Still, why would he need the fae woman?"

Jasmin snapped her fingers. "She was magical, like most supernaturals. He could have been using her; which would account for the payments to her."

"He wasn't using her," said Torie. "They were working together."

"That would also explain why Wednesday said they hadn't spoken in some time. Her mother led us to believe that she had recently cut off communication. That was why she wanted her found. But if they weren't on speaking terms…" said Jasmin.

"Then she needed Wednesday for something as well," finished Torie.

"Jeez. She was using her own daughter for who knows what," said Fionna. "Little did she know, if she had just waited, her daughter would have come to her. Wednesday wanted to hide out at her house after all."

Torie and Jasmin exchanged glances.

"She didn't know Wednesday was in trouble or headed home. But the warlock did. He slept with her. No way that was a random encounter, and I'm betting he also knew exactly who she was," said Torie.

"So many connections. But I'm still having a problem seeing the whole picture," said Jasmin.

"So what do we tell Wednesday?" asked Torie.

"We tell her the truth; what we know so far, which isn't a lot," said Jasmin. "She deserves to know her mother was involved with the warlock on some level and that she may have been using her as well."

"Of course she was," came a voice from behind them. Wednesday had been standing quietly in the living room listening to the conversation. She walked into the room.

"I wasn't trying to eavesdrop. I just came down for some tea. Not the drugged kind from last night…just the regular kind."

Torie arched both eyebrows and felt redness creeping into her face.

Wednesday held up a hand before she could say anything.

"Forget it. If I'm being honest that was the best night's sleep I've had since all of this began. Plus, this baby is kicking up a storm; so it put her little butt to sleep as well."

"You know it's a girl?" asked Jasmin.

Wednesday nodded. "Yes. Call it fae intuition. But I'm one hundred percent it's a girl."

"So you heard what we were talking about?" asked Torie as she set about filling the kettle. "We don't mean to speak ill of your mother. I hope you didn't take it that way."

Wednesday took a deep breath. "Look, I'm not perfect. As a matter of fact, I'm probably a pretty awful person. I'm selfish, spiteful, arrogant and materialistic. I do what I need to do in order to get what I want out of life. Where do you think I got that from?" She paused, looking at the women. She dunked a tea bag in a steaming cup of water that Torie handed to her. "My mother was not a nice woman. She may have pretended to be salt of the earth, but she was far from that. She had her own ambitions. She was just too afraid to go out into the world and get what she wanted. I saw that in her and vowed I wouldn't be like her. I wanted the means to live the kind of life I always dreamed about."

She turned and looked at Torie. "When I met Ward, I saw my chance. And I took it, without thinking twice. Even if it meant destroying someone else in the process. I didn't know you at the time. That made what I did justifiable in my mind."

She tried to ignore the look of disgust on Fionna's face, but it was impossible. She turned to face the shifter, her eyes growing moist.

"Say what you want to about me. I deserve it," said Wednesday.

"I was going to say, do you still feel that way?" asked Fionna.

Wednesday sipped at her tea. "No. But I don't know why. But if I had to do it all over again, I'd like to think I'd make a different choice." She looked down at her baby bump. "I want to be a better role model for this one than my mother was. Of course, it won't matter if I end up giving birth in jail."

Torie walked over and put a hand on Wednesday's shoulder. "No one's going to jail. And for what it's worth; I owe you. Without you, I wouldn't be here in this town I've come to love. And I wouldn't have these friends I've also come to love." She looked at Fionna and Jasmin and smiled.

Just then, Fionna's phone buzzed, and she pulled it out of her back pocket, swiping at the screen. Her eyes grew large, and she looked up at her friends, fear clouding her eyes.

"What is it?" asked Torie.

"It's from Eddie," she said. "He's texting for help. He said there is a man at Arnold's right now, that he's trying to cast some kind of spell on him."

Chapter Seventeen

Fionna was fretting in the back seat as the three women sped through town.

"Maybe we should have brought Elric," she said. "I mean, he's tussled with the warlock before. Plus, he's really strong."

"And that's why he needs to stay at the house," said Torie. "He needs to protect Wednesday and her baby in case something goes wrong."

"And by go wrong, you mean in case something happens to us," Fionna whispered.

"Nothing is happening to us," said Jasmin. She whipped the car dramatically through the streets and past slower vehicles.

Torie closed her eyes. She had been working on devising spells that would allow her to go on the offense if needed. Her lips moved as she committed incantations to memory. She remembered the touch of the warlock's magic when she and Elric had been attacked.

There was a rawness to it that terrified her. It wasn't like the magic she felt when she worked with Jasmin. Their practice sessions had been in harmony; calling on the forces of nature that were all around them.

Jasmin had taught her to control a lot of her power. Her natural telekinetic gifts as well as her skill at manipulating fire. That one she had inherited from her mother. Alva had been a master at generating fire balls and controlling flames, Jasmin had said.

That would definitely come in handy now. For the most part, her magic hadn't worked when she was fused with Elric. Jasmin was right; without being able to speak, she was limited in what she could do. The werewolf also didn't have human hands that she could use to make mystical gestures that could summon power.

But she was in her own body this time. She was prepared. Or at least she hoped she was.

"So, what's the plan?" asked Fionna. "For when we get there, I mean."

Jasmin chanced a quick look at Torie and shrugged.

"Don't die," she said, her voice deadly serious.

"What if this guy latches onto one of you? Can he siphon off your magic?"

"I've been thinking about that," said Jasmin as she made a sharp right onto the street that led to Arnold's law office. "I don't think it works like that. In order to drain our power, the warlock would most likely need us unconscious and not fighting back. Then he could use his own black magic to take our power. So that's part two of the plan; don't get knocked out." She gave Torie one more glance before coming to a screeching halt in front of the office.

The three of them hurried out of the car and raced up the stairs to the front door. Torie tried the handle, only to find it was locked. She banged on the door with her open hand, calling out Arnold's name. Silence greeted them.

"Come on," said Jasmin. "Let's try the back door."

"I'll look for another way in," said Fionna as they stepped off the porch. She shifted to her squirrel form and scampered up the side of the Victorian to the second-floor roof line and vanished across the dark shingles.

Torie and Jasmin ran to the back of the house where a private entrance welcomed them under a striped red and yellow awning. The door was solid wood that had been painted black, clashing with the house and the awning above.

Jasmin tried the door, only to find that it was locked as well. She placed a hand on the lock and whispered a single word. Torie heard the tumblers turn, releasing the lock. Slowly the door crept open and the two of them entered. It was eerily quiet inside, and just like the rest of the house, the windows were all shut with large, blackout shades drawn.

"Arnold?" called out Torie.

Jasmin grabbed her arm quickly, silencing her before she could call out again. She placed her forefinger on her lips and nodded for Torie to follow her quietly.

The back entrance opened into the large kitchen. There was a back stairwell that led to the upper levels of the house. Jasmin looked at Torie and nodded.

Taking a clue from her friend, Torie stretched one hand outward and whispered. She waved her fingers and tiny wisps of blue smoke snaked forward, creeping up the staircase. Torie stood her ground for a moment and then shook her head at Jasmin. The trail of smoke returned to her, flowing back into her open hand.

There was no one, living or undead, upstairs.

They made their way out of the kitchen, down the back hall to the main business entry of the home. They knew beyond that they would find the stairs that led to the basement vaults. They both knew that if Arnold were here, that was where they would find him.

"What about Fionna?" Torie mouthed to Jasmin.

"She'll find us," she replied in silence.

They moved slowly towards the back stairs. Torie clenched tightly onto Jasmin's arm. Now she was regretting not asking Elric to follow them. Why had she been concerned for Wednesday's wellbeing? She was sure if things were reversed, she was still certain Wednesday would not worry about Torie's safety. But that was what made them so different. No matter what she had done, Torie wasn't about to leave a pregnant woman defenseless.

Even if she was a conceited home wrecker.

They stopped at the top of the stairs and peered down. They exchanged looks and each took a deep breath. Jasmin flipped up the light switch on the wall, but the sconces did not light up.

"Great," she breathed.

Holding up a hand, she summoned a glowing ring of light that illuminated the way for them.

"Stay behind me," she whispered to Torie. "And if anything goes sideways, run. Don't worry about me."

Yeah right, thought Torie, *like that would happen.*

Locked together, they made their way into the basement, moving by memory as they tried to decipher which way to go. They knew that the vault with all the safe deposit boxes was dead ahead, but beyond that, they were lost in the cavernous space.

"Which way?" asked Torie.

"I don't know. I've only been to the vault before. I don't know where his private chambers are."

Torie closed her eyes.

"Spirits that dwell in this place most forbidden,
show us what this vampire keeps hidden."

A shimmer passed through the darkness, and immediately the walls around them became translucent. It was like looking through a wet shower liner, but they could make out the shape of things hidden in rooms all around them.

To their left was a chamber that caught the witches' attention. There was a raised dais in the room with what looked like two coffins sitting atop it.

Exchanges glances, they approached the wall that concealed it. The spell Torie had cast was fading, but they were able to find the part of the wall that contained a hidden door. Jasmin pushed against it with her magic, commanding the door to give way before them. The space they entered was enormous, sprawling out in front of them. It was outfitted with antique furniture in various states of disrepair.

Beyond the dais where the coffins rested, there was an enormous four-poster bed that sat alone.

"Why would he need a bed if he sleeps in a coffin?" asked Torie.

Jasmin looked at her. "Coffins are a bit tight for certain activities."

Before Torie could respond, she felt something wet drop onto her face. She raised a hand and rubbed at her cheek. Pulling her hand back, the liquid appeared bright red in the glow cast by Jasmin's magic.

Blood.

They looked up simultaneously and gasped as one.

There, on the ceiling, clung Arnold. He supported Eddie in one arm, holding the shifter's neck to his mouth as he drank.

Jasmin screamed as she aimed her light at them, willing the intensity of it to brighten to a degree that she hoped would momentarily blind the vampire. He screeched in return, dropping Eddie as he leapt from the ceiling to floor, landing in a crouch before the two witches.

Eddie hit the floor with a sickening crunch, lying motionless as blood quickly pooled around him from the wound on his neck.

"Arnold?" said Jasmin, backing away slowly. "What are you doing? What have you done to Eddie?"

The vampire hissed, his eyes shining black as he bared his fangs. They weren't the pearly white, pointed ones Torie once pulled from his head with her magic. No, these were long and mismatched, the ends of them more blunt and jagged. They more resembled tiny saw blades that glinted black in the light.

"Arnold, it's us…it's Jasmin. Do you remember me?"

Again, the vampire hissed, taking a step toward them.

Torie held out her hand, palm up, and opened her mouth to speak.

Arnold moved faster than anything she had ever seen. His form became a blur; one minute he was standing across from them, the next he was inches away from her face, one hand closed around her throat, choking off her air supply.

"Not this time, witch," he said. His breath was fetid and warm on her face.

Torie looked into his eyes and knew that he was no longer in control of himself. She kicked her feet wildly as she felt him lift her into the air. She struck out blindly with her fists, to no avail. It felt like she was being held by a piece of living steel.

Jasmin ran to her side. Placing one hand against the side of Arnold's face, she unleashed a blast of magic that caused the vampire to roar in pain. He relaxed his grip on Torie's neck as he swung out at Jasmin, clipping her with the back of his hand and sending her across the room to crash against the large bed.

He turned his attention back to Torie, bringing her back up to face level. He forced her head to one side, exposing her neck, and leaned in, licking his jagged teeth.

A wet, popping sound that reminded Torie of when she used her mallet to tenderize chicken reached her ear, and Arnold's body stiffened, his head snapping backwards as he dropped Torie to the floor, staggering backwards.

He looked down at the pointed end of a large wooden stake protruding from his chest.

The undead creature turned slowly to see the face of Fionna behind him. He grabbed at the stake before smiling at the horrified shifter.

"Thank...you..." he managed, before falling to the ground, his body disintegrating into a red ash that scattered around them.

Torie's lungs burned as she sucked in oxygen, trying to make her way to her feet.

"Check on Jasmin," she managed, her voice raw and weak. She pointed to the bed and her friend's crumpled figure.

Fionna ran to the fallen witch just as she started to come to, moaning at the pain radiating from her shoulder, down her left side.

"Oh my God, are you okay?" asked Fionna, helping her to drag herself up onto the edge of the bed.

Jasmin nodded. "I will be. Just got the wind knocked out of me."

"That was more than wind," said Fionna, pushing a stray strand of black hair from Jasmin's eyes.

"Where…where's Arnold?" asked Jasmin. She followed Fionna's eyes to the smoldering ashes along the floor.

Torie came over to them, rubbing her neck.

"Fionna…are you okay?" she asked.

The shifter nodded, but then emotion overcame her, and she buried her face in her hands, tears flowing as she ran from the room.

"C'mon," said Jasmin, taking Torie's hand, "let's get out of here."

They started to move but were stopped by the sound of a low moan coming from the floor next to the bed.

"Jesus, it's Eddie," said Torie, hurrying to his side. "He's still alive."

"Barely," he murmured.

He was right. Blood was flowing from an open wound in his throat, and his body was already growing cold.

"We have to help him," said Torie.

"I don't know that we can," replied Jasmin. She crouched down, taking his hand in hers. "Eddie, the man you called us about? Was he the one who did this? Did he do something to Arnold to make him do what he did?"

The young shifter nodded, clawing desperately at Jasmin's hand. His breathing was short and labored, his eyes moving about the room quickly, not focusing on any one thing. He grabbed at his throat, making gurgling noises as he pulled at the women around him.

Tears streamed down Torie's face as she held his hand. He squeezed gently, his body contorting as he tried to point at something, his slowly graying eyes trying to focus on something in the room.

"What is it, Eddie?" Torie asked softly.

He gurgled, jutting his chin in the direction of the coffins.

"The coffins? Is that what you are trying to say?" asked Jasmin.

He nodded once, then his body grew still, his eyes unfocused as his last labored breath escaped him.

Slowly, the witches stood up and walked over to the two coffins. Both were covered by heavy, elaborately carved wooden lids.

Jasmin summoned a ball of light then looked to Torie, nodding. Together, they lifted the first lid to reveal an empty space, lined in red velvet. They moved over to the second, took a deep breath, and opened that one as well. It, too, was empty.

"I don't get it," said Jasmin, looking around. "Why would he need two coffins? Eddie was obviously human, so he wouldn't sleep in one."

"Maybe he was going to turn him?"

"Maybe. Though from what I know about Arnold...the Arnold I knew...he would never have done that. He hated what he was and would never wish that on anyone else."

They headed back to the stairs when Jasmin turned to Torie.

"We need to call the police. Let them know that Eddie's body is here."

Just as she finished the sentence, Torie's phone vibrated in her pocket. She reached for it, looking at the number that popped up.

"It's Max. Fionna must have had the same idea and called him." She swiped at the screen and placed it to her ear. "Hey, Max. We were just about to call. Did Fionna tell you what happened?"

She stopped talking, her brows furrowing as she listened.

"What is it?" asked Jasmin.

"Okay, sure. She's at my house. We'll meet you there." She hung up, returning her phone to her pocket. "Max wasn't calling us about all of this. He said he just got a report from the county morgue. A body has gone missing."

Jasmin looked at her friend, a feeling of dread creeping up her spine.

"It's Allira. Wednesday's mother."

Chapter Eighteen

They found Fionna sitting in the back of the car, and for the entire trip back to Torie's house, she did not speak.

As soon as they pulled into the gravel drive and eased the car to a stop, she climbed out and walked slowly toward her own vehicle.

Torie hurried to catch up to her. She placed a hand on the shifter's shoulder and made her face her. Neither of the women said anything, but Torie grabbed her and pulled her in tight for a hug.

"I am so sorry you had to experience that," she whispered.

Fionna's body went limp as she started to cry again. "I thought...I assumed that if it ever came to it, and I had to do that, I'd feel better. Feel some kind of relief about avenging Taylor. But I didn't. I feel terrible about what I did. I didn't even hesitate. I must be just as bad as he was."

Torie placed a hand on the back of her head, stroking her lightly.

"No, Fionna, you are not. Sometimes, good people have

to do bad things. If you hadn't taken action and did what you did, Jasmin and I would probably not be here now. I, for one, am thankful for you."

Fionna backed away to arms-length, wiping the wetness off her face.

"I'm going to go home now. I need a long hot shower followed by a giant glass of wine with Glen holding me in front of the fireplace."

"That sounds divine. You do that. I'm going to call you later to check in, okay?"

Fionna nodded and turned to walk away.

"Thank you again, Fionna. And I know I speak for Jasmin as well."

Fionna offered a half smile and nodded before climbing into her car and pulling away.

Torie headed back to the front porch where she joined Jasmin.

"Is she okay?"

"No. But she will be. What about you?"

Jasmin didn't speak, her eyes focusing on something in the distance. "I will be too."

It was all she could offer as they both walked into the comforting warmth of Torie's home. They made it to the couch and plopped down. Torie held out a weary hand, calling for a bottle of whiskey and two glasses to appear. She poured each of them a stiff drink, passing one to Jasmin.

"Max should be here soon," Torie said. "That should be fun."

"Why is he coming over?" came a voice from the second floor. It was Elric, and his footsteps let them know he was none too happy to have overheard what he just did.

"Eavesdrop much?" said Jasmin, taking a gulp.

Elric took one look at them and overwhelming concern flooded his features as he rushed to Torie's side.

"What happened to you? Are you okay?" He reached out and took her hand. "It feels like every time you leave the house without me lately, I end up asking you the same things."

Torie smiled, her heart warmed by his worry.

"I'm fine. Really, we're good."

Elric looked at her, his eyes zeroing in on her neck and the darkening bruise that encircled it. His eyes flared yellow, and she could feel the animal rising in him.

"Damn those bloodsuckers," he said, rising to his feet. His voice deepened as he curled his hands into fists. "I'm going to kill that monster."

"Too late for that," said Torie, reaching for him to hold her hand. "Fionna beat you to it."

His stance softened and his eyes reverted to their normal color as he calmed down a bit.

"Fionna? Was she hurt? Where is she?"

"She's gone home. I think she just needs some time to herself," said Torie. "But listen, Max is headed over. Are you going to be okay, or do you need to go back to your place for a while?"

"I'm not leaving your side," said the werewolf. "But I would like to know why he's coming here."

She told him everything that happened, ending with the frantic call she had received from Max.

"He wants to speak with Wednesday about something. Where is she by the way?"

"Napping," Elric said. "She looks different. Her body has...changed within the last couple of hours."

Torie started to ask what he meant, but the doorbell

rang before she could. She went to get up, but Elric held up one hand, moving to open the door himself.

He swung it open to face his old Alpha.

"Max," he said, his voice a little more than a growl.

"Elric," said Max, his own voice a mix of surprise and annoyance. "I didn't know you would be here."

"Indeed," said the beta. They faced one another silently for a moment before he stepped aside, allowing the sheriff to enter.

"Christ," said Jasmin. "I thought the two of you were about to whip out right there to break the ice." She rolled her eyes and returned to the amber liquid in her glass.

"Thank you for coming over, Max," said Torie, ignoring everyone else in the room. "Before you tell us what's going on, we need to let you know about something that just occurred at Arnold's."

For the second time, she found herself retelling the day's occurrences.

"Aren't you going to take notes?" she asked, looking at the small flip pad he kept in his vest pocket.

"No," he replied. "I'm learning there are some things that happen in this town that are better off not having a paper trail." He turned his head to the side and spoke briefly into the communications headset that was fastened to the shoulder of his uniform. "I just dispatched one of my deputies to the scene. He knows how to take care of certain situations that require discretion." He stole a quick glance at Elric. "I trust him completely."

Elric bristled but refused to be baited.

"Anyway, I'm not going to lose sleep over a dead vampire," said Max.

Now it was Jasmin who bristled. "How dare you. Arnold

was my friend. And no matter what you might think, he was a good person."

"Maybe you need to rethink your friends then," he replied. "That friend killed an awful lot of shifters, in case you forgot."

Torie felt magic well up within Jasmin. She immediately sat forward, placing a hand on her friend's shoulder.

"Okay, let's all just take a breath before we say-" she looked at Jasmin, "-or do something, we'll regret in the morning."

Jasmin took a deep breath and sat back, reaching for the bottle of whiskey to pour herself another two fingers.

"Max, tell us what happened with the body of Wednesday's mother," said Torie.

He took another long look at Jasmin before turning his attention to Torie.

"Like I said. Her body is missing. It was at the morgue on ice, and now it's vanished. I got a call earlier about a disturbance at the morgue. My deputies were all out patrolling. I was bored, so decided I'd take the call myself.

"As soon as I walked into the place, I knew something was up. The place smelled like fresh blood. And death. I followed the scent of blood to where it was strongest...the body bay. The attendant who had originally called in the disturbance was dead. Throat had been slashed. That was where the smell of blood was coming from.

"Then, when I entered the actual bay, I could see the door of one of the body wells had been pulled off the wall. It was the bay that housed the fae's body. But the body was gone."

Torie thought about what he had said.

"Was the door pulled off from the outside or was it forced open from the inside?" she asked.

Max thought for a moment. "Not sure how it makes a difference."

Jasmin bolted upright. "No, Torie's right; it does make a difference. Think, what did you notice?"

Max searched his memories of the scene. "The way it was buckled...it looked like it had been punched off its hinges; so yes, it was forced from the inside. But how is that possible?"

Torie and Jasmin exchanged looks.

"Two coffins," said Torie.

"Yep. Now we just need to know why," said Jasmin.

"We need to know more than that," said Torie. "We need to know where she is."

"What are you talking about?" asked Elric, chiming in.

"Elric, can you go get Wednesday? We need to speak with her. It's important," said Torie.

He nodded and made for the stairs.

"Yeah. Go fetch," said Max out of the corner of his mouth. Elric growled in response but made his way up the stairs.

"Okay, enough," said Torie. "The two of you need to kiss and make up, or whatever the hell wolves do when they've had a falling out. There is a lot of serious shit going down in the town right now, and I can't have my boyfriend feuding with his ex-bestie."

Max raised his eyebrows.

"Boyfriend?" he said. "So it's serious, huh?"

Torie blushed and looked around.

"Don't look at me," said Jasmin, folding her arms. "This is the first I'm hearing about this." Although the twinkle in her eyes said she had her suspicions.

A creak caught their attention, and they turned to see Wednesday coming down the stairs.

Torie nearly blinked in comical surprise at the sight of her. She had indeed changed. Her face had lost its sharp, angular features. It was now fuller, her jawline slightly less pronounced. Her flaxen hair was now more frizzed, with streaks of purple beginning to show through her dark locks. Her frame was definitely heavier as well. She was carrying more weight, especially in her limbs. Her stockiness made it difficult to walk down the steps.

"Oh great. Another one," she said, eying Max as she dropped heavily onto the couch.

"Wednesday, are you okay?" asked Torie. "You look a little different."

"What?" she said, looking down at her body. "Never seen a fae approaching full term with a baby before?"

Not only was her jaw less pronounced, but Torie could have sworn that her features were becoming harder, less soft around the edges. Pregnancy did strange things to the human form, who knows what it did to a fae.

"Actually no," said Jasmin, squinting to get a better look at the fae. "It's quite fascinating."

"Mind your business, witch," said the fae, adjusting the robe she wore around her. "So, what is it? The mongrel said you needed something."

"Hey," said Max, "that mongrel is a wolf. And don't you forget it."

Wednesday rolled her eyes. "Look, what do you need? Because I hear a hot bath calling my name."

"Wednesday, we don't think your mother is dead," said Torie. "Well, at least not in the way you might be thinking."

Jasmin stepped in, seeing the questioning look in her eyes.

"We were just at Arnold's. He...he killed Eddie, his lover. We are pretty sure the warlock was behind turning him back into the same savage creature that killed all those shifters a couple of months ago."

Wednesday crossed her legs, her foot nervously swinging back and forth. "So? Vampires don't need a reason to go savage. It's their nature."

"She isn't wrong," said Max.

"Well, we also have reason to believe he was involved in some way with your mother," continued Torie. "That key your mother gave you opens a safe box that Arnold's law firm keeps for certain supernaturals here in town. Ones that need to keep certain activities quiet."

"There was a ledger in that box. It detailed payments to an account your mother had. Payments that were shared with Breonna, the hedge witch the warlock was using to control Arnold. In Arnold's personal space, we found two coffins," said Jasmin.

"So what? You did just say he had a lover."

"His lover wasn't a vampire. He was a shifter, but not a vampire. He wouldn't sleep in a coffin. Also, Max made another discovery today," said Torie, turning to the sheriff.

He cleared his throat. "Your mother's body is gone from the morgue. And as weird as it sounds, evidence points to the fact that…the body tore its way out of the freezer."

Wednesday huffed. "What, you think my mother, a fae, is now a walking undead, prowling the town? Don't be ridiculous."

"There's one other thing," said Max, taking out his cell phone. "Something I haven't even told you yet." He looked at Torie and Jasmin before swiping open his cell and pulling up some pictures. He handed it over to them before continuing. "There were marks all over her arms and legs. Puncture wounds that looked like they were continuously healed over and then re-punctured."

"And you're just now thinking this might be of interest to us?" said Jasmin, annoyed.

"Hey, the medical examiner was still trying to figure out what was going on when...well, today happened."

Torie studied the pictures. "Could these be bite marks? It almost looks like something...or someone, was feeding on her."

Wednesday looked at the pictures, her face a mask of disgust.

"I'm sorry you have to see these," said Max.

She waved him off. "Don't worry about it. My mother and I weren't that close. But these marks, they aren't bite marks. I've seen this before."

"What is it then?" asked Torie.

"Fae blood has specific properties that are known to possess healing powers. At least the fae that are born with a sensitivity to magic. We live a very long time, and our blood has been known to pass that ability on to other supernaturals."

"But vampires live just as long, if not longer," said Elric. "They don't die...so why would Arnold need your mother's blood for that?"

"It wasn't for him," said Jasmin, thinking aloud.

"The warlock," said Torie. "It was for him."

Jasmin nodded, then turned to Wednesday. Something on the young fae's face caught her attention.

"What is it, Wednesday? What do you know?"

The fae said nothing at first, but then let out a long sigh.

"My mother was getting something out of it. She was getting money, probably a lot of it. And she also would have gotten the one other thing she desired most."

"What's that?" asked Torie, prodding her to continue.

"Youth. Or, to be more precise, the continued appearance of youth. My mother was one hundred and twenty-five years old. But she looked like she was just approaching mid-forties. That's how life is for fae. We age, but much slower. My mother was always obsessed with her looks."

"You think she would have made a deal to have Arnold change her?" asked Jasmin. "That would have kept her looking the way she did...forever."

Wednesday nodded, not looking up at anyone in the room.

"But what about the money? Why would she need that? I saw her home...she was not living outside of her means by any stretch of the imagination," said Torie.

"That would have been for me," Wednesday said. "She always wanted me to stay here, to be with her. She used to say that one day she'd find a way to have enough for me to be happy. I never believed her; never imagined she would do this. What I wanted was for me, and I intended to make my own way. But she always told me that one day...she'd have what I needed to come home."

The fae broke off, the last words getting caught in her throat.

"So she was working with the warlock and Breonna. He paid Breonna to supply him with shifter parts for his experiments, and he paid your mother for her blood, to keep his magic up, no doubt," said Jasmin.

"And then you two come along and seriously throw a monkey wrench into his plans by killing his hedge witch before he was ready to do...whatever he had in mind," said Max.

"But if all this is the case, then there is still one piece that doesn't fit in," said Torie. "If he had your mother under control, why would he risk getting involved with you?"

Wednesday shrugged. "Like I said, *I* went after *him* that night."

Torie shook her head. "He just happened to be in that bar at the same time you just happened to go into...whatever sends you into heat? And you just happen to be the daughter of the woman he's getting his magic fix from? No. There has to be a connection."

Jasmin snapped her head around to stare at Wednesday. "Didn't you say that in your family, magic skips a generation? Your mother has it, right? But you don't?"

"Yes, that's correct," said Wednesday.

Jasmin looked at her, then down at her belly.

"Christ," said Elric. "You don't think he's after the baby, do you? Would he really use his own kid like that?"

"He's a warlock. And Wednesday said he told her he was after the holy grail of magic the night they slept together. Who knows what that meant."

There was a creak on the stairs behind them, and all heads turned to see Ward standing there. His face was emotionless as he stared at Wednesday, a single tear falling down his cheek.

Chapter Nineteen

"Come on," said Torie, "I think we need to give them some space." She motioned for the others to follow her out of the room, only to be stopped by Ward.

"No, that's okay," he said, walking slowly the rest of the way down the stairs and into the room. "Seems like everyone already knows a lot more than I do about whatever is going on. Might as well continue the conversation in the open."

Wednesday had a panicked look in her eyes. She bit her lower lip and cast a pleading eye Torie's way.

"No, this isn't something she needs to speak about for you," said Ward. "I mean, she's just the bitch ex-wife as you used to call her, right?"

"Ward, please. Let's go somewhere we can talk," Wednesday said.

He shook his head. "No. Something tells me that wouldn't be a good idea." He looked around at the rest of the people in the room. None of them would meet his eye. "So, what was that about you sleeping with someone else?"

Wednesday blushed, and despite herself, Torie felt a pang of sorrow for the fae.

"Ward, there is a lot you don't know about this town, and about Wednesday," Torie said.

"Yeah, I'm starting to realize that." He looked at Max. "So, what are you?"

"I'm a werewolf; same as Elric," he said softly.

"Of course you are. Why not. My ex-wife is a witch and is now dating a wolf. Why wouldn't she pal around with other witches and monsters?" He turned to Wednesday, his eyes red and moist. "And you?"

"You know me, Ward," she said.

"What about our child? What is it? For that matter, is it...mine?"

She didn't speak, which was all the answer Ward needed.

"I'm out of here," he said, making for the door.

"Ward, no! Wait," she said, struggling to rise from the couch. "There is nothing that I can say to make this right. All I can offer you now is the truth...about any and everything you want to know. Just, please don't leave me. Until you've heard everything."

He stopped in his tracks, turning to face her, his body shaking.

"What, Wednesday? Give me a reason not to walk out that door."

"Because I love you. Honestly. Openly. Fully. In a way I have never felt before; in a way that I didn't know was possible."

Slowly, painstakingly so, he walked back into the room. Max and Elric moved aside, letting him face his girlfriend.

"I'm not of your world, Ward. I wasn't born into it. And I probably shouldn't have ventured into it; but I did. I met you, and, well, things took off. I knew you were married, but I also knew how you were feeling." She glanced at Torie, her eyes offering apologies that she didn't have words for.

"I am a fae. We live on instinct and in the moment. My instinct told me that you felt about me the same way I did about you. And that first night that we…you know…I was enthralled. All I wanted was to be in your world, no matter what it meant. I wanted you and everything that you could give me. I goaded you on when we talked about how we could make even more money; even though it meant hurting others.

"But as I said…I'm fae. There are certain things about my people that you couldn't understand. One of those is the drive to reproduce. It's frowned upon, but we can do it with human males. But in your case, it wasn't possible. On account of you being snipped and all." She stopped, studying the floor, unsure how Ward would respond to that.

"I…I don't even know how to respond to that," he said. He turned, focusing his attention on Torie. "And you've known about this? Been a part of it since we arrived? I knew you'd be mad at me, Torie, but I had no idea you'd take part in making me look like this big of a fool."

"No," Torie responded. "You do not get to say that to me. *I* made *you* look like a fool? You have no idea what I have been through since you walked out the door on me. The guilt I have felt; first over our marriage failing and then about the people in our community who trusted you…trusted *us*…and what you did to them? Some of them are ruined for life, Ward. I was the one who had to face the media back home. I was the one who had to sit there while helicopters circled our home as the government hauled away everything we owned to try and pay restitution for the mess you created.

"You walked out on your son, Ward. Then you show up here, looking for safe harbor, not feeling an ounce of guilt over what you did. Not feeling anything at all until now… when you find out that the woman you left your family for cheated on you." She was trembling now, but no tears came. Her rage was hot, and she felt she was long overdue for this release.

"You were a part of my life at one point. But not any longer. Do you know what it's like to finally admit to yourself that the one person you loved more than anything in this world, never loved you back? There is no place for you in my mind or my heart anymore. I refuse to give your presence real estate in my being. I don't want you here. You are no longer welcome, Ward. My anger at Wednesday was misdirected; *she* wasn't married to me. She didn't make vows stating she would always be there. You did. And you broke them." She turned to face Wednesday. "I'm sorry that you hitched your wagon to a piece of shit like this, but you did. His karma is now yours, and I feel sorry for what is probably headed your way.

"Tomorrow, I want you out of here, Ward. I'll give you a thirty-minute head-start before I call the FBI."

No one moved. The silence was deafening, and had someone spoken, Torie was sure she would not have heard them over the sound of blood rushing around her ears.

She couldn't look at Ward, and she had to be careful what she thought. Unlike Wednesday, she was pretty sure he wouldn't survive being engulfed in flames.

Jasmin stood and walked over to her friend. She didn't say anything. She didn't have to. She stood by her and took her hand, letting her strength and resolve flow into Torie, letting her know that she was there for her no matter what.

Torie gave her hand a squeeze in acknowledgment and then released her.

"Whiskey," she said, holding out her hand. A glass that was barely touched appeared in her hand, and she sipped it, ignoring the stare that Ward gave her.

"Well," said Wednesday. "I have to say I'm not surprised by any of this. I've been alone most of my life, I can certainly handle this alone as well." She started to point to her stomach, but stopped, her brow furrowing. "Ouch! What the hell was that?"

"What is it?" asked Torie.

"The baby…just did what felt like a somersault. And… oh no…oh no…" She stood and bent double, cradling her mid-section. "I think it's time!"

For a second, no one moved. Then pandemonium broke out as everyone started barking orders at one another and trying desperately to figure out what to do.

"Okay, stop!" said Torie, standing in the middle of the chaos. "Everyone just shut up and calm down." She turned to Wednesday. "Except you. Should we get you to the hospital for this?" Wednesday shook her head, eyes wide and pleading. "Fine. Ward, help her to my bedroom and get her into the bed." Torie then turned to Jasmin "Call Glen, get her over here as soon as possible." Immediately, Jasmin took out her phone and made the call.

"This is going to sound really weird, but I think we need a major shielding spell around the house. We still don't know what this warlock is up to, but if he was able to sniff me out when I was merged with Elric, chances are he will certainly be attuned to a fae birth like this. Especially with it being his child."

"I'm on it," said Jasmin, leaving the room.

"You two," said Torie, pointing to Max and Elric. "I

need you patrolling outside. Nothing comes near this place that isn't Glen. For all we know there is a newborn vampire out there prowling around."

The wolves looked at one another and grumbled.

"Okay this," said Torie, waving one arm at the two of them, "stops right now. I couldn't give a shit about who hurt whose feelings. Right now, shake paws and make up. Then get out there and start sniffing for trouble."

Max's eyes widened as he turned to face a smiling Elric.

"I'm sorry I didn't join your deputies," said Elric before Max could speak. "I know it hurt you, but it wasn't that I wanted to abandon you; I knew you'd be fine. I just needed to make my own way, clear my head of all…that we went through over the past years. Leave all that darkness behind and start fresh. With that amazing woman over there."

"Oh my God," said Torie, shooing them out of the room. "Have that conversation outside. I've got things to do now."

The two wolves exited the room and went out the front door, closing it behind them.

Once everyone was out of the room, Torie looked around. Now what was it that she needed to be doing?

Oh yeah, she thought, eying her glass of whiskey on the coffee table. She picked it up, downed it in two gulps, and headed into the kitchen. There she began heating water, and then went to the storage closet to retrieve as many clean linen pieces she could find.

She had no idea what any of these things were for but knew they were always asked for in television shows whenever someone went into labor outside of a hospital.

That fact caused her mind to begin wandering. Why would anyone in their right mind not want to go to a hospital to have a baby? They had drugs there. And those amazing epidural needles that numbed everything. Who would pass that up?

Someone wanted by the government, that's who.

Surely Wednesday would be safe at the community hospital here? No one would dare try to turn in a member of the community. Only Wednesday wasn't a member anymore. She had turned her back on this place, and in a community like this, there was no coming back from that.

Torie thought for a minute. Maybe, if they couldn't take her to the comforts of the hospital, they could magically bring the comforts to her. Glen would do what she could, of that Torie had no doubt; but there were certain things she knew the nurse would not be able to give.

Like hard drugs and epidurals.

She shook her head, trying not to think about those. Women had been having babies for centuries the natural way. Modern medicine was relatively new.

But what was the mortality rate among those women centuries ago?

Again, she banished those thoughts from her mind. Maybe, there would be something she and Jasmin could do to make the birth easier on her. Not that she cared about Wednesday per se, but if they made it easier on her, then it would also be less traumatic for the child as well.

A knock at the door took her mind off magical deliveries and thoughts of what kind of spells would be needed for the act. Glen had arrived.

Torie heard Jasmin and Fionna talking with her and walked into the living room.

"I didn't know what to do so I boiled some water and got some clean linens," she said to Glen.

The nurse smiled nervously at her. "Thank you, Torie. I

grabbed what I had at home, but you do know this is going to be rough, right? Truthfully, I don't even know what to expect. I've seen plenty of deliveries, but never a fae one before."

Torie nodded. "None of us do. But Jasmin and I are ready to provide any kind of magical assist you need."

"I am definitely going to take you up on that."

"Okay, grab the linens and come on up to the bedroom. Be sure to not let them touch anything. They're to wrap the baby in, and they need to be as clean as possible. Torie, you get the water and bring it. We need to let it cool and I'll use it to clean the baby."

They both nodded and went back into the kitchen.

"Isn't this exciting?" asked Fionna, her previous qualms forgotten. "A new baby fae is coming into the world. In your house no less."

A scream from the master bedroom rattled them both and they hurried out of the kitchen and down the hall. Torie reached the bedroom first, bursting through the doorway to see Ward lying on the ground, his head bleeding.

She looked around, but there was no one other than Glen in the room with him. Glen was bent over his body, slowly turning him over. He moaned loudly, his eyes fluttering wildly.

"Ward, what happened?" asked Torie.

"It was Wednesday. I helped her into the bed, covered her, and then turned around to find you and...she must have come up behind me. But she moved so quietly that I didn't even hear her. I heard her whisper she was sorry, and then it felt like I was hit with a baseball bat. That's all I remember."

Torie looked around to see that the large window in her

room had been opened. She stuck her head out but didn't see Wednesday.

"She took off," said Torie.

Ward winced, brushing off Glen's attempts to dab astringent on the wound to the back of his head.

"I'm fine," he said. "Where is she? You have to find her."

Torie looked at Ward, searching a face she thought she had known for a lifetime. There was no deception in his eyes, no lie betrayed by his features. Whatever he had felt in the heat of their argument, one thing was certain; he was afraid for Wednesday and her unborn child.

He loved her. And that moved Torie in a way she never would have imagined possible.

"Don't worry, Ward. I'm going to get her back, safe and sound. I promise."

She told Glen to look after him, then told Fionna to come with her.

"Go find Jasmin and tell her we need to leave," said Torie. "I'm going to get the wolves and I'll meet you at the car."

"Where are we going?" asked Fionna, heading for the door.

"The only place she could have gone. Home."

Chapter Twenty

They had all piled into Max's police bronco. It allowed him to speed through town without attracting too much attention. He drove with Jasmin riding shotgun. Fionna, Torie and Elric sat in the back.

"How many guns do you have?" asked Torie, looking at Max's reflection in the mirror.

Jasmin whirled in her seat. "Why would you ask that?"

"Because we have no idea what we are walking into. Chances are, there could be a vampire and a warlock waiting on Wednesday at her house."

"We don't even know for sure that she will be there," said Jasmin.

"Where else would she go? She thinks everyone, including the man she loves, has turned on her. She will go to the one place she feels safe." She clenched her jaw, staring at the blur of trees they passed. "And if her mother is what we think she is...who knows what an undead fae is capable of."

"Probably something that bullets can't stop," said Fionna.

"No, but they might slow her down. And if the warlock is there, they should work against him."

She looked at Jasmin, who just returned her stare. Torie knew what she was thinking. That this wasn't like her. She didn't believe in violence as the only means. But she also knew when there were little alternatives.

There were two lives at stake. One that hadn't even had a chance to start out in this world just yet. If violence and bloodshed were the only way to ensure the child had a future; then so be it.

"Well at least this time you're not going in alone against who knows what," said Elric. He had been strangely quiet, and when Torie had gently pushed at his mind to inquire what was wrong, he had only smiled and gave her hand a squeeze. Still, he remained silent, and Torie respected him too much to pry further.

"We're coming up to the spot where we'll have to start walking in order to get to the fae's house," said Max, slowing the SUV.

None of them were looking forward to the trek through the woods in the dark. Not with a warlock and a potential vampire on the prowl.

What had been beautiful and inviting during the day, was now dense and foreboding in the darkness.

"Jasmin, can you throw some light on things for us?" asked Torie. "Not all of us can see in the dark."

"Probably a good thing," said Max, looking over at Elric as they made their way into the forest.

"What do you mean by that?" asked Torie, glancing around nervously.

"Don't worry about it," replied Elric. "Let Max and I take point."

The two wolves moved to the front, shielding the three women behind them. Something about the way they moved made Torie anxious. The sudden warm glow of red light that emanated in a ball from Jasmin's hand set her feeling at ease almost immediately.

"That's better," said Jasmin.

Something to their right skittered away from the glow, diving into the cover of shadows behind them. Torie and Fionna started, grasping hands as they continued moving towards Wednesday's house.

"This doesn't feel the same," said Fionna. "Something is not right."

"Agreed," said Max. "We are being watched."

Just then, a shadow broke free from beside them, and a slim figure rushed out of the woods, throwing itself at the group.

The shifters reacted far faster than the two witches could have imagined. Fionna shifted to her squirrel form, and in an instant both wolves were leaping at the shadow, shifting on the fly.

Max and Elric landed the first blow on the creature, each snapping down on something that crunched under their jaws. A scream of pain rang out briefly but was quickly silenced by a bite from Max's powerful jaws.

Jasmin and Torie approached carefully when whatever had leapt at them stopped moving. It lay on the ground, gray and hairless in Jasmin's mystic light.

"What is it?" questioned Torie.

"Vampire," said Elric, shifting back to human form. "Or at least it will be. It's a newborn that hasn't fed yet. Until they feed for the first time, they don't have much form or shape. Just the lifeless blobs they become when they are first infected by another vampire's bite."

"This one was out hunting for its first taste of blood," said Max. "They aren't hard to kill when they are like this. But once they taste blood, it's a whole different ball game."

Fionna stood next to the wolves, staring down at the creature. Her nose quivered and she backed away.

"This was a shifter of some kind," she said, her voice cracking. "How is that possible?"

"Whatever bit this one is a completely different kind of vampire. Its bite worked on a supernatural. That shouldn't be possible," said Max.

"Unless the vampire was part supernatural itself," said Torie.

Jasmin nodded. "A fae."

Elric and Max stiffened, their bodies turning to face behind the group.

"Run," Elric said to the women. "Get to the house… and no matter what you hear, don't look back."

Before anyone could protest, he and Max shifted and began to charge at something that was approaching from the rear. They roared their defiance as one, and Torie could hear the snapping of their powerful jaws as they disappeared from the edge of Jasmin's light.

"You heard the man," said Jasmin, turning and heading for the house as quickly as she could, "Move it!"

Torie cursed her knees and they cursed her right back for forcing them to run over the uneven ground. She found herself silently swearing she would get back to the gym once this was all over.

If she lived that long.

As one they burst into the small clearing that led to the front of the house. Something squatted on the low roofline, barely visible in the dim light. As they approached the front porch, it leapt down at them.

Jasmin gestured, the light she cast turning solid and bouncing the creature away into the darkness. Torie spun to face the door, fear causing her mind to go blank so that she shouted the only spell she could think of.

She slammed both hands at the door while saying, "Open sesame!"

The door flew open under the power of her magic, and the three of them poured inside, with Jasmin slamming the door closed behind them. She concentrated, moving her arms up and outward before the opening, sealing the door with magic as well as locking it from the inside.

They were bent over, hands on knees, sucking hard for air. Only Fionna seemed unfazed by the physical exertions they had just put themselves through.

"What now?" she asked, looking around.

Jasmin huffed, forcing herself to stand. "I really need to workout with your trainer."

"Oh, I don't have one," said Fionna.

"Bitch, that was rhetorical," said Jasmin, placing her hands on her hips as she started to recover her breath.

A scream echoed throughout the space, raising the hairs on the back of Torie's neck.

"That came from the back of the house," she said, running in that direction. They passed by the kitchen, and she held out her hand. "Knife!" she said, feeling the cold steel handle of the butcher blade as it flew to her.

The house was laid out like the old row houses she had seen once when she was visiting a friend in Philadelphia. It was narrow, but long with each room built off a central hallway that ran the length of the structure from front to back.

The hall ended at the master bedroom and behind that was the master bath. They heard loud panting, punctuated by moans and more screaming coming from the bathroom.

Calling up her magic, Jasmin led the way, followed by Torie and her knife and Fionna.

The bathroom was lit by dozens of candles that gave off heat and created an eerie flickering that Torie found disturbing. In the center of the room was a large sunken bathtub.

The tub was full, overflowing onto the floor. Wednesday sat in the tub, the water up to her chin. Her hair was plastered to her head, but Torie couldn't tell if that was from the water or the sweat that seemed to be pouring down her face.

"Wednesday, what's going on?" she demanded. "Why did you leave?"

Wednesday squeezed her eyes shut and let out a long groan through clenched teeth. Then she began panting rapidly.

"Isn't it obvious?" she breathed. "You're going to hand my baby over to who knows what. Ward couldn't care less. I'm all alone here, and I'm not giving up my child. I've made a ton of mistakes but giving away a part of me won't be one of them."

She screamed, her hands gripping the top of the tub.

"Jeez," said Jasmin, "how far apart are your contractions, Wednesday?"

The fae panted heavily a few times before she could answer. "I have no idea. Something is happening…I just need to get this thing out of me."

Fionna was at their side, trying not to stare at what was going on but also wanting to get the witches' attention.

"There's something in this house," she whispered. "I don't know what it is, but the smell is nauseating."

"Wednesday, look at me," said Torie. "Who's here with you? We can't help you if we don't know everything."

The fae looked at her, eyes dark and fixed as she stared at the witch.

"What do you care? You're free to take your husband back now if you want him."

Torie started. "Is that what you think is happening? Trust me; I have no interest in Ward." She swallowed hard and looked the fae in her eyes. "He loves you now. I've seen it in him."

Wednesday's breathing caught in her lungs, and before she could respond, she screamed again, pitching her head forward.

"Okay, we can discuss this later," said Torie.

She reached out both hands and placed them on either side of Wednesday's head.

"Spirits of the moon that wax and wane,
help me soften this suffering and pain."

A soft glow suffused the water around the fae, and slowly, she relaxed her grip, settling back into the bathtub.

"What...what did you do?" asked Wednesday.

"Not as much as I'm betting Glen could have done with her bag of medicine if you had stayed at the house."

"Thank you, Torie...but the baby?"

"The baby will be fine. I just wanted to..."

That was as far as she got. The water around Wednesday began to bubble up around her. Almost as if someone had just turned on the jets in a jacuzzi.

Wednesday threw her head back and screamed as the pain she had been feeling returned two-fold.

"Oh my God, what did you do, witch?" she screamed.

"Nothing…I was trying to help!"

Jasmin stepped in at that moment, placing both hands in the air above the tub.

"It's the baby," she said, her eyes closed. "You magic isn't working on it. If anything, it's fighting back. It's immune to your spells…"

Fionna backed up into the women at that point. "Guys, whatever is in this house is moving around out in the hall."

She was pointing to the shadowy opening that led to the hall. She turned to look at her two best friends, and then at Wednesday.

"Take care of her," she said, before running out the door, closing it behind her.

"Fionna, wait!" cried Torie, moving towards the door.

"No," said Jasmin. "She can handle herself. We need to get this baby delivered and out of here safely."

Wednesday's screams were now low, guttural cries that escaped between rapid exhales.

"How?" asked Torie. "Magic doesn't work on her. What now?"

"What do you mean how? We let nature take its course and then…I don't know, cut the umbilical cord and send her on her way. Why are you asking me this? You're the one who's had a baby before."

Torie's face lit up. "You're right. I have been through this."

She sat down next to the fae.

"Wednesday, when you left my house, had your water broken yet?"

The fae shook her head, grimacing and trying to breathe through the pain.

"Okay, so it broke here. That means we could still have quite a bit of time before the baby comes."

Again, she shook her head, reaching to grasp Torie's hand.

"No, that isn't the case for fae. When our water breaks it means we are ready. Typically, we give birth in rivers. That wasn't an option for me so I ran a bath hoping the water would help. But something isn't right." Again, she threw her head back and screamed in pain.

A loud thump, followed by the sound of breaking glass and someone yelling came from somewhere in the house. Torie tried not to think about Fionna out there fighting for her life against who knew what kind of monster.

No. She couldn't let herself think about it; there was work to be done in here.

"I thought you sealed the house?" she said to Jasmin.

"I did. But if someone was already in here, then…"

"Then they're trapped with us."

"It's my mother," Wednesday said between breaths. "She was here, waiting for me. She knew I'd show up eventually."

Torie and Jasmin looked at one another, concern for their friend now mounting.

"Is the warlock here?" asked Jasmin.

Wednesday shook her head and grunted, her face a mask of pain and fear. "Why isn't she coming out?"

"Why a river?" asked Torie. Jasmin looked at her questioningly. "What is the importance of a river? Why can't the fae just give birth in a pool or something?"

"My mother said it had to do with the fact that all fae are born surrounded by water and the flow of the river helps to pull it out...or something like that. She was supposed to be in here, but then she heard you all tromping through the woods and left me here."

"Okay, none of that makes sense," said Jasmin. "Studies have shown that water births for human females really don't do anything to help the medical outcome of the mother or the baby."

"Maybe. Maybe not. But the one thing it does do is reduce the stress on the mother's body. It's easier for her to move around in water than lying in a bed. We have no idea how fae physiology works, so maybe the water has some sort of effect on her that allows the birth to happen easier. But it has to be moving. Hold her hand, I'm going to try something."

They switched places, with Torie now standing and Jasmin holding Wednesday's trembling hands. Torie held out both arms over the tub and began to move them concurrently over the water. She moved slowly, her whole body waving in a push-pull motion.

"What are you doing? You look like those ladies in the park practicing Tai Chi in the mornings," said Jasmin. "Magic doesn't work on this child."

"I know. But it will work on the water."

She began to exaggerate her movements, sweeping her arms high into the air and away from the tub. Almost at once, the water began to rock in the large tub, following along with the pull of Torie's magic. It began to swell and recede, rocking upward out of the tub and then settling back down, crashing gently against Wednesday, rocking her body in time with Torie's sweeping arms. Wednesday moaned softly in response, relaxing her death grip on Jasmin's hand.

"Whatever you're doing, it seems to be helping," said Jasmin. "Keep it up."

Another bang in the hallway, followed by the sound of flesh striking flesh. Whatever was happening out there was getting closer and closer to the bathroom.

Wednesday leaned forward in the rocking swell of water, grasping her knees with both hands. Jasmin placed a hand on the fae's back to help support her, gently encouraging her to push.

She timed the pushing with the retreat, the pulling away, of the water, and then gasped in a deep breath as the water pushed back in against her. Together, she and Torie built a rhythm; deep breath in surrounded by warm water, hard exhale and push when the water retreated.

Suddenly, Wednesday's dark eyes rolled back in her head until only the whites showed. She threw her head back, face to the ceiling, and screamed at the top of her lungs. The tub filled with light, swirling in large golden circles that breeched the surface, breaking free of the water in large floating bubbles that glowed so brightly Torie could barely look at them.

The bubbles were tiny, reminding Torie of the time her family had visited one of the bioluminescent bays while on vacation in the Maldives. It might have been beautiful if it weren't blinding.

But then, as quickly as it started, everything stopped. A single golden ball floated free of the water, but unlike the ones that came before, this one was amorphous, swirling and changing shapes. It also had a dark, solid core. Something inside moved about, pushing at the sides of the bubble.

Torie gasped and reached up, catching hold of the

bubble as it floated away from her. It was warm to the touch, and very slick. It was like holding a large water balloon made of light. Torie squinted, staring at the solid mass in the center of it. Slowly, she recognized a tiny hand, and then a foot as it pushed against the sides of the water bubble it was cocooned within.

"Break it!" cried Wednesday, panting. "She can't breathe."

Torie wasn't sure what to do but acted on pure instinct. She held out her hand, calling for the knife she had brought with her from the kitchen. Then, being as careful as she could, she inserted the tip into the ball just enough to collapse it with a small pop. Water fell from the construct, splashing to the floor, along with the knife that Torie dropped.

In her hands, she now held a beautiful baby girl, one with slightly pointed ears, enormous blue eyes, and skin the color of copper. The baby yawned and stretched in her hands before looking up at the woman who held her. She smiled, stretching out a tiny hand that grasped at the air in front of Torie in an effort to reach her hair.

"Oh my God...she's so beautiful," said Torie.

Wednesday leaned forward, her arms outstretched. "Can I have her please?"

"Of course," said Torie as she offered the newborn to her mother.

That was when the door smashed open, flying off its hinges to crash on the far side of the bathroom.

"Not so fast. I'll be taking that baby."

In the doorway, stood Wednesday's mother. Her skin gray and nearly translucent. She smiled, her tongue flicking at her pearly white fangs. She held out one hand for the baby, and in the other, she held the unconscious Fionna aloft by her neck.

"Or would you rather I snap your friend's neck?" said the vampire.

Chapter Twenty-One

Torie hesitated, looking to Jasmin for a clue as to what should happen next.

The fae backed up slowly, motioning for them to follow her with her free hand.

"Bring the child and follow me," she said. "And don't think for a minute I won't kill your friend here."

"Torie, no, please give me my baby," said Wednesday, pleading with the witch.

"Uh-uh," said her mother, "you do that, and you might as well say goodbye to Squirrel Girl here. And your four-legged boyfriend."

With that, she slipped out of view, moving out of the hall toward the open part of the house.

"Wait here," said Torie. "And don't worry, nothing will happen to your baby. I promise." She followed Jasmin out of the bathroom, her heart breaking as she shut out Wednesday's cries of anguish. She could hear the young fae trying to get out of the bathtub, her movements feeble and lacking in any coordination.

Jasmin didn't say a word as they headed for the living room where the fae stood, still holding the unconscious Fionna.

"First," said the fae-turned-vampire, "You're going to drop the shield around the door. And remember, even though I'm vampire now, I am still fae. I can sense magic, and if you so much as whisper an incantation in my direction, I will break her in two."

Jasmin looked at Torie, who just nodded, holding the baby close to her chest. Jasmin gestured to the door, whispering a single word as she waved her hand before her. The door shimmered with energy as a ripple passed from it to the witch's outstretched hand. As soon as Jasmin released the protection spell, the door splintered inward.

A man, tall with incredibly pale skin, stepped through. He was dressed in jeans and a black long-sleeved t-shirt. His face was sharp and angular with a nose that was so defined it looked like the beak of a bird. His eyes were purple and crackled with dark energy.

Stolen energy, thought Torie.

As he entered, he dragged something behind him in both hands. A thump resounded through the space as he dropped two unconscious figures.

Elric and Max.

Torie gasped, instinctively taking a step in their direction.

The warlock held up a single hand, ticking his forefinger back and forth at her.

"Not so close," he said, smiling. "At least not yet."

The man strode across the room and stood beside the vampire fae. He wrapped an arm around her and kissed her passionately on the mouth, never taking his eyes off the witches. The vampire fae moaned softly, dropping Fionna to the ground as she wrapped her arms around him. When they broke their kiss, Torie could make out a slight bridge of red spittle stretching between their lips. The warlock reached up with a thumb and wiped away the blood from his bitten lip.

He smiled as he licked at it, acutely aware of how it made the witches feel.

"So much power in the two of you," he said. "You've no idea how badly I've wanted to meet you both in person." He waved a hand in the air, his fingers tracing delicate circles. Purple sparks of light crackled around him, tearing away like cobwebs before a broom. "Umm. You taste delicious. But there will be time for that later."

He focused his eyes on the baby in Torie's arms. She drew the child closer to her protectively and took a step back, increasing the distance between the two of them.

"What did you do to Elric and Max?" she asked, looking at the two men on the floor.

The warlock laughed. "Probably the same thing I'm going to do to you and your friend. Well, I'll go further with the two of you. Shifter magic, especially that of werewolves, is not the most desirable. It will do in a pinch, like getting a hot dog from that rotisserie thing at a cheap gas station. You know it will stave off hunger, but you also know you'll have a case of the bubble guts later on. But you," he closed his eyes and sniffed the air, "Are five-star Michelin all the way. I knew it when I first ran across you in the woods. Even buried inside that wolf, you were magnificent."

"So that *was* you," Torie said.

"Of course. You burned so very brightly; I was intent on having you right then. I wasn't expecting you to be able to lash out with your magic while in that body. But it also gave me an idea of what you can do; I won't underestimate you again."

His hands were clasped behind his back, and before anyone in the room could react, Jasmin threw a ball of blue light in his direction. He whirled, holding up a hand and laughing as the light exploded harmlessly against him, hitting an invisible force field that he projected. Waving his hand, he sent Jasmin tumbling across the room.

He turned nonchalantly, facing Torie.

"As I was saying. I came prepared for this." He winked at the fae. "As I'm sure you guessed, I've been siphoning magic from the fae for some time now. But once she became one of the undead, her magic also died. She cannot sustain me any longer. Lately, she has been resorting to summoning shifters to us so that I can feed off them. And then, she feeds off them, turning a few and setting them free in the woods." He turned to the unconscious wolves and pointed. "I believe they ran into some of them tonight. Then they ran into me…and well, you can see the result of that."

"Did you kill them?" asked Torie. She couldn't tell if they were breathing, and the thought of that was making her see red.

"No. Not yet at least. I knew I would need them as bargaining chips. A trade if you will." He focused his unearthly gaze on the child in Torie's arms.

Torie shook her head, taking another step away.

"You can't," she said. "She's your own flesh and blood."

The warlock looked at her then the baby. He shrugged.

"Exactly. That was the idea," he said. "In this case, magic is like an organ. The closer you are to being a genetic match, the less likely the chance of rejection in the event of a transplant."

"What are you going on about?" said Jasmin. She was

slowly making her way to a sitting position, holding onto the side of her head.

"What does any warlock want?" the man said.

"Oh, I don't know, finally move out of his mama's basement and actually work up the nerve to talk to a real girl? Finally throw out the sock with lipstick on it he keeps hidden away?" answered Jasmin.

The warlock sighed before thrusting out his hand in her direction. He closed his fist violently, and in response, Jasmin felt her throat begin to close. She reached for her neck with both hands, her eyes wide with fear.

"See, if I wanted to suck the considerable magic out of you right now, I could do that. But it would eventually run out. It would only power me for so long. What any warlock wants is to become self-sustaining. No need to borrow power from other magical entities."

"The holy grail," said Torie.

"That's right," he said, turning to face her and releasing his hold on Jasmin. "Very good. I seek the holy grail. And in that little bundle of joy, I've found it."

"Since you're being so talkative, I assume you'll tell us just how that works?" She was stalling, and the warlock sensed that.

"If you're thinking that your wolf friends are going to wake up soon and save you, think again. I sucked enough energy out of them, they may not wake up till tomorrow. If they're still alive at that point. And that depends entirely on you handing over the child."

"I promised her mother I would protect her." Torie's mind was racing. Magic was her only weapon, but she wasn't sure there was anything she could do to hurt the warlock. She had barely survived their first encounter; and she was afraid of confronting him while trying to protect an infant. She looked pleadingly at her friend.

Jasmin raised a hand and started to mutter an incantation but stopped when she saw the vampire fae place her foot on Fionna's neck.

"If it will help you any, the baby won't feel anything. I needed something that generated magic that I can make my own. A force that doesn't fight me like with magic or shifter energy. Fae's are born with incredible potential. Power that is raw and untapped. It fades of course as they get older, but when they are first born, they are truly wondrous creatures of nature. This one is imbued with my own personal essence. The magic it generates is something that I can claim and use as my own. Indefinitely."

"And you?" said Torie, looking at the vampire fae who was standing on Fionna. "You're okay with this? With him using your daughter and now your granddaughter like this?"

"Whose idea do you think this was?" said the warlock, smiling at the vampire fae. "Her understanding of magic goes far beyond what you witches comprehend. You are born with the ability to control forces that you never bothered to learn about. I am going to do things that you can't even begin to imagine."

"Mother...is that true?"

The vampire fae turned to see Wednesday standing behind them in the hallway. She was dressed in a white gown that clung to her wet form. She leaned against one of the walls to support her weight, one hand cradling her midsection. Her dark eyes held those of her mother's.

"Were you using me?"

"Oh, come now, Wednesday. Do you really want that child?

I wasn't using you…but, well, I could not have children with him, but I knew you could. And because magic skipped you, I knew any child you had with him would be very powerful."

Wednesday stared at her mother, her mind racing.

"Did you summon me here? When I went into heat… was that your doing?"

The vampire fae smiled. "Yes, dear. All of it. I drew you here, and I triggered your heat cycle. I gave the warlock the power to cast a glamour on himself so he looked like the human you had been seeing. I taught him the potion he slipped you that night in the bar to make you more…receptive to his advances."

"You did this to me…all for money?" said Wednesday.

"Oh, and this," said the newborn fae, baring her fangs. "I am eternal now. No more aging for me."

"You're disgusting," said Wednesday, turning to the warlock. "Do what you want with me, but don't hurt my child."

"Ha," he replied. "I have no more use for you. Still, I will grant you this one mercy. Go back to your room until this is over. I won't force you to watch what I am about to do here. Afterward, I'll let your mother turn you. You'll see things differently after that."

"No," she said softly. "I've seen and heard enough." She let the stake she had been holding in her sleeve slide into her hand, which she tossed into the air.

"Now, Fionna!" she screamed.

The shifter opened her eyes, looking up at the surprised vampire fae. The creature increased the pressure on Fionna's neck, meaning to snap it, but before she could, Fionna shifted to her squirrel form and slipped from under the vampire fae.

Once she was no longer underfoot, she leapt into the air,

shifting back to her human form on the fly. Holding out her hand, she caught the sharpened stick in one hand as she landed behind the monster. Her shifter-enhanced speed wasn't as fast as a vampire's, but at that moment, it was enough.

She struck before the vampire fae could turn, plunging the stake into her back, rupturing through her still heart.

Wednesday's mother was dead before she knew she had been struck. She slipped to the floor, a look of confusion on her face as she melted away.

"That's for putting them dirty hooves you call feet on my face," Fionna said to the ashes before turning to face the warlock.

"How dare you?" he screamed, his eyes flashing hotly.

He held out both hands and sent a wave of power emanating outward in all directions, blasting the women against different walls within the house.

Torie screamed as the baby was torn from her arms. The infant did not crash to the floor as expected, however; even as she was flung back, the child floated in place, suspended in a bubble of purple magic.

The air was knocked out of her and her vision blurred as she saw the baby floating over to the warlock. She struggled to her knees, looking for Fionna and Jasmin. They had been closer to the warlock and took the brunt of his blast. Neither moved as they lay on the floor against the far wall.

Torie focused her energy and called for the knife that she had when she was in the bathroom. It appeared in her hand as she struggled to her feet.

She held out one hand and sent a bolt of fire screaming at the warlock. It struck his back, only to dissipate into nothingness.

He turned, smiling at her. He held the baby in one arm,

the crackling field of magic that surrounded them both seemed impenetrable.

"So much energy in this one," said the warlock, holding two fingers over the child's head. "Its immunity to magic is protecting us both now: even as I prepare to drain her. You might as well save your energy; no magic or supernatural being can harm me now."

He returned to looking down at the child, drawing on dark forces as he began to chant, summoning what looked like a glowing dagger to appear over the child.

"No!" screamed Wednesday as she clawed her way across the floor towards them. "Please don't do this! Not my baby…please!" Her face was a mask of terror and fear for her child. She knew there was nothing she could do; her child was about to be sacrificed by a madman.

Torie cried out, her own words carried away by the din of dark magic that was forming around the man.

She didn't know what to do. She summoned her magic to try another attack, but the words of the warlock rang out in her mind.

"No magic or supernatural being can harm me…"

She stopped, letting her magic subside. She knew what she had to do. But would it work?

She closed her eyes, focusing her willpower as she spoke.

"A human I once was, a human I'll yet be,
small and powerless, when I count to three.
1-2-3."

On three, she clapped her hands together forcefully as she sent her magic ripping through her body. Instantly, she felt weak as she dropped to her knees. Whether it worked or not, she had no idea, and she did not have time for a field test.

Scooping up her knife, she ran at the warlock. The magic that crackled around him gave way before her as she moved in close to him.

He turned to face her at the last moment, but it was too late. She was on him and drove the blade of her knife deep into his chest. The warlock's power flared like a flash bulb once again, but this time it hurt no one. He slumped to his knees, and then onto his side.

Torie snatched the baby out of mid-air before it could fall and stumbled away from him. It was over in little more than the blink of an eye. She stood there, a shocked look on her face, holding a newborn over the dead body of a warlock.

Chapter Twenty-Two

The sunrise breaking over the meadow and making its way through the canopied treetops was beautiful. Dappled patterns of orange and yellow flowed into the front of the house, warming the space and helping to chase away any lingering ghosts that clawed at the memories of those who were still breathing.

Glen was there, giving the newborn its first check-up. Ward stood close by, watching the infant have her lungs and heart listened to. He chewed at the fingernails of one hand, waiting for Glen's evaluation.

"She is perfectly healthy from what I can tell," she said to Wednesday. "She's ready to feed, if you are up for it."

Wednesday's eyes lit up. "Yes, I need to do that." She stood up, and Glen escorted her and Ward to one of the private rooms at the back of the house.

"I'll be back in a minute to check on you two," she said, nodding at Elric and Max. They sat on a couch, battered and bruised, but already beginning to heal.

"You fought well," said Max, looking at his old beta.

"I'd forgotten how fearless and strong you are," replied Elric. "It was nice. Not the almost dying part, but the two of us being on the same page again."

Max smiled and slapped his friend on the back. The impact made them both wince.

"How is she?" said Max, looking across the room at Torie.

"She's strong. Whatever is happening to her; we will deal with it. Together."

Torie could feel his eyes on her but she could not bring herself to look at him. She sat in a chair, a tattered blanket around her shoulders. Jasmin had pulled a small ottoman up to the chair and sat facing her, holding both of Torie's hands in hers.

"Torie, what have you done?" she asked.

Torie swallowed and shook her head slowly. Her eyes were unfocused and fixed on a point that was halfway between them.

"I didn't think. All I knew was that I couldn't let that monster hurt that innocent child. I did what I had to do."

Fionna stood next to her, lightly stroking her hair.

"You saved that baby. You saved all of us," she said.

Jasmin nodded. "I've never seen anyone perform such an act of selflessness like that."

Torie could tell by her tone that she wanted to say something but couldn't bring herself to voice it. She looked at her friend and forced a weak smile.

"Yes, Jasmin, it's gone. My magic. I can't feel it at all."

Jasmin blinked rapidly, and Torie could tell she was fighting back tears.

"You don't know that, Torie. You're a witch; you were born to have these powers. They can't be gone."

Torie had told herself that right after the dust had

settled and everyone started to regain consciousness. She thought maybe it was temporary.

Why oh why hadn't she used a spell that made it temporary?

Because she didn't have time to think it through, that was why.

Glen walked back into the room and approached them slowly.

"The baby's eating, and Wednesday seems to be fine. The wolves are all bandaged up; but with their healing I think they would have been fine without my help." She looked at Torie and offered a slight smile. "I would offer, but I don't think I have anything in my med kit that will help you. I'm sorry."

Torie smiled. "Thank you for everything, Glen. As always."

Glen turned to walk away but was stopped by Fionna's hand on her arm.

"Hey, what about you? Are you okay?" asked Fionna.

Glen glanced at Torie and Jasmin before turning to her wife. "I'm fine. I'm just...Fionna, it scares me now; anytime I see your number light up on my phone. I don't know what horror may have happened to you. I mean, in my mind I think 'is this Fionna calling or one of her friends to tell me something awful has happened to her'. Is this what our life is going to be now? You being attacked by who knows what and me getting a call to put you all back together again?" A tear ran down her face that she quickly wiped away. "I'm sorry. I'm just tired. It's been a long night. I need to get some rest. I'll see you at home." She turned and walked out of the building, bag in hand.

Fionna looked at Torie and Jasmin, hands raised in a

shrug that begged for their guidance as to what she should do next.

"What are you waiting for?" whispered Jasmin to her. "Go after her...now! We'll be fine cleaning everything up here."

Fionna gave one last look at her two friends before nodding sharply and running out the door after Glen.

"Are they going to be okay?" asked Torie.

"They'll be fine. All relationships change over time. But that one is as solid as they come." She turned to face Torie. "But now we need to work on you."

Torie shook her head. "Jasmin, I don't think there is anything we can do. I just...I just need to get home and think this through. Maybe Mom can-" She caught herself mid-sentence. "Oh God...I had been thinking that I was going to try and figure out a way to get my mother back... but now, without my magic, that won't be possible. I've lost her forever."

She was too shocked to cry this time. All she could do was stare into the kind eyes of her friend and allow a sadness she had not known in ages to wash over her.

"Excuse us," said Wednesday as she walked into the room, carrying the baby, with Ward trailing behind them. "I just wanted to say thank you again for what you did. She wouldn't be here if it weren't for you."

She leaned forward, showing them the sleeping face of a baby girl with jet black hair and ears that were slightly pointed and curled against the side of her head. To Torie, the child looked perfectly angelic; and just like that, all the self-pity she was feeling went away.

"She's beautiful," said Jasmin. "Have you thought of a name yet?"

Ward and Wednesday exchanged a nervous look.

"Well," said Wednesday, "we were hoping…I mean, if you're okay with it, we'd like to name her Torin. After the woman who saved her life."

Torie felt her eyes well up. The lump in her throat told her not to trust her voice at the moment. All she could do was nod; and that was enough.

Wednesday began to slowly bounce the child in her arms, turning back towards the bedroom with her. Ward stayed behind, looking at Torie inquisitively. He looked at Jasmin nervously.

"I know I don't have a right to ask, but can I speak with Torie in private? Just for a minute?"

Jasmin glared at him. "Hmph. Only because I have a call to make." She got up and left the room, heading out the front door.

Ward cleared his throat. "She told me what you did; what you sacrificed. Why'd you do it, Torie?"

She smiled at him, took a deep breath, and thought of her mother.

"Because, Ward, sometimes you just know when you're doing the right thing."

He nodded and was about to make his way back to the bedroom before stopping and giving her a serious look.

"I want you to know, I'm heading back to Westchester. I'm turning myself in."

Of all the things Torie had just experienced, this might have been the most shocking to her. She looked at him questioningly.

He couldn't meet her gaze and stood there scratching his head sheepishly.

"These last few weeks have shown me what my life is going to be like. Running from place to place, trying to stay one step ahead of the consequences that are coming as a result of my actions. Even if we made it out of the country, I'd still be running. If it were just me, then I might risk it; but what kind of life is that for Wednesday and a newborn? No, I can't do that to them. I've already reached out to our lawyer about coming in. Part of the deal is going to be that I take full responsibility for everything. Wednesday, and you, are spared any further investigation or charges."

Torie didn't say anything, just watched the man whose actions had simultaneously upended her life and given her a new one.

"You have an amazing second life here, Torie. You deserve to live it peacefully."

"What about Wednesday? Will she be staying here in Singing Falls?"

He shook his head. "She said there is another community like this one out west, near San Francisco, that is a little more her speed. She's heading there as soon as she's up to it."

"Good for her," said Torie. "And Ward? One last thing. You need to speak with Shawn this time, before you leave."

"I doubt he wants to hear from me after what I did."

"Maybe. Maybe not. But one thing's for sure, if you don't talk with him, then he will most definitely never want to hear from you in the future."

Ward smiled and nodded. He turned and walked slowly back towards the bedroom, leaving Torie alone with her thoughts. Maybe doing the right thing was contagious. That thought made her smile and helped ease the pain of losing her magic. It was strange that she could feel so hollow from losing something she had only had for such a short time. But in that time, it had made her feel whole. No, more than just that; she had felt like she had a purpose at last.

She let out a deep breath as she realized that life wasn't

over. She would find a new purpose. She was still part of a great community, and she had the best friends a woman could ask for.

Life would go on, and she would as well.

She snapped back to reality just as Jasmin walked back into the room, ending a phone call she was on and slipping her cell back into her bag.

"You are not going to believe what Ward just told me! He's turning himself in! He's willing to go to jail."

Jasmin waved a hand to cut her off. "Girl, ain't nobody got time for that. He *should* be in jail. I have better news." She gave her a mischievous grin.

"Okay," said Torie, her interest piqued, "are you going to tell me or is this a guessing game?"

"I just left a message with my sister in New Orleans."

"I never knew you had a sister. Why didn't you tell me?"

Jasmin shrugged. "We aren't the closest. But I think she can help with your problem."

Torie looked away, brow furrowed. "Jasmin...I don't think anyone can help me."

"Well if anyone can do it, she can. She's a witch doctor. And I'm going to make her come here and help you. Don't give up on hope just yet, my friend."

The two older ladies sat outside of the bakery sipping their coffee and passing the time with idle gossip. It was a beautiful evening, the crisp mountain air was invigorating, and, as two fox shifters, they enjoyed the various scents that floated to them on the breeze.

The sight of the large black diesel truck that rolled to a

stop not far from where they sat on Main Street didn't draw their attention.

The young woman who climbed out of it did, however.

She was barely in her twenties they guessed, and from the way she was dressed, she definitely wasn't a native. She wore a white crop top that bared her midriff, revealing a row of chiseled abdominals. Black leather pants that seemed uncomfortably tight and completely weather inappropriate, and a corded leather belt with a silver buckle complemented the line of silver snaps on large, clunky boots. She carried a black leather jacket slung over one shoulder, and in her other hand she clutched a dark green backpack.

Her face was half hidden by too-large, rose-colored sunglasses. Her brown skin seemed almost golden in the setting light of the sun. Dark, natural hair that was pulled into two massive afro-puffs on either side of her head completed her look.

She looked around before turning to the driver of the truck, thanked him for the lift, and closed the passenger side door. As the big vehicle roared off, she slipped her glasses down lower so she could peer over the rims, taking in the picturesque downtown area.

She sighed deeply as she started down the sidewalk, never looking into any of the small town shop windows as she passed, and not giving the two old shifters that stared at her a second glance.

As soon as she passed, each of them frantically pulled out their cell phones and made calls.

"Well," said one of them to someone on the other end, "there goes the neighborhood. Looks like a hunter has come to town."

The hunter stopped as she reached the end of the street,

pulling out her own buzzing phone. She swiped upward, placing it to her ear.

"Yeah, I made it. You sure this is the place? It looks like something out of a Hallmark Christmas movie; boring as hell." She nodded, rolling her eyes. "Whatever. Just deposit the money in my account and send me the picture of the targets. But I'm telling you, this place does not look like werewolf central."

She tapped at the phone, ending the conversation. Seconds later, two texts came through. The first one was from her bank, showing that her fee had reached her account.

The second, was a picture of two men standing in a bar. She had no idea who the men had pissed off to get such a bounty on their heads, and truthfully, she didn't care.

The advance they offered her had cleared and she now had a job to do.

She closed the phone as she crossed the street, having committed their faces to memory. Now, all she had to do was find the ones known as Max and Elric.

"Alright," she said to herself. "Two dead werewolves coming up."

vinci-books.com/toriehex

There is never a good time for a witch to lose her powers.

Torie Bliss gave up her magic to save a life—just when darkness descends on Singing Falls. With a supernatural war brewing, a Hunter on the hunt, and no powers left, Torie must prove that even powerless, she's still a Hex Witch.

Turn the page for a free preview…

How Torie Got Her Hex Back:
Chapter One

Torie sat cross-legged on the floor, staring at the fireplace. Then she looked over at the pieces of wood she had brought in, which were stacked next to an old newspaper.

"How the hell do you even make a fire?" she wondered to herself. In her previous life as a married woman, she made fire by pressing a button, and watching the gas ignite the crystals in her modern style fireplace. But how do people actually do it with sticks and paper?

Just a week ago, she would have issued a mental command that would have caused the wood to ignite, filling the living room with warmth and light. But that was before.

Before she sacrificed her powers to save the newborn baby of her ex-husband's fae mistress.

Now, she was forced with the seemingly impossible task of replicating the first thing early man created in order to survive: fire.

She sighed, reached for the newspaper and crumpled it, creating a bed in the fireplace. Now, do you light it and then put the wood on top, or put the wood on, then light it? It made more sense to do the former in her mind, but that didn't mean it would work. She only had one newspaper, and therefore, only one shot.

In the end, she decided to stack the pieces of wood on top first and weave more crumbled pieces of paper between the logs.

Satisfied with what she saw, she reached for the starter lying on the mantle and lit the paper. Slowly, the fire she created made its way between the logs, lighting them as it went.

Pleased with herself, Torie smiled and made her way to her feet. Her knees had progressed from creaking to giving slight pops that were echoed by the sharp exhales of breath as she stood. The floor was now her enemy; along with the ottoman, the couch in the spare room upstairs that was way too deep.

She made a mental note to check out the only gym in town later in the week. With the coming cooler air, her joints were already starting to protest, beginning when she swung her legs out of bed in the mornings and not letting up until she made her way back into said bed that night.

Why hadn't she tried to magically fix that when she still had her powers?

"You know why, Torie. Because you had no reason to think you'd ever lose your magic."

She made her way to the kitchen and poured herself a shot of whiskey to sip. She could have waited until Elric had come by and asked him to make her a fire, but wasn't that something, along with bathing and feeding herself, that she should be able to do on her own? Besides, she liked having a fire. The crackle was soothing in the ever-present silence of the house.

Had it always been so quiet? She tried not to think

about her mother. That path would take her someplace dark, and that was the last thing she needed. No, she needed to put on her happy face. Her friends would be coming by later to check in on her, and she had to convince them she was alright.

Food.

That was what she needed to focus on now. Put out a spread so they would see she was in a good place.

Except that she wasn't. The thought of taking out pans, prepping food, baking and sautéing...all things that she truly loved, was exhausting. Instead, she went to the pantry, retrieved some mixed nuts and tossed them into a large service bowl. Then she took out a few different cheeses, cut them into small blocks and arranged them on a platter with some thin sliced cold cuts.

Instant charcuterie.

The spread was sad compared to what she would normally present, but given her current state of being, she was pleased with the outcome. Wine and a few bits of chocolate that she placed around the living room would have to be enough, she decided. She looked at the wine; two bottles of red. She went back to the liquor cabinet for a third.

That would be for her, she knew.

Everything was ready, and that left her plenty of time to get herself together. Making her way to the master, she poured over the simple dress collection she had acquired since moving to Singing Falls.

Her wardrobe was far simpler than what she had possessed when she lived in New York. But unlike before, her clothes now matched how she felt. Breezy, colorful, lightweight sundresses. Jeans that didn't threaten to cut off the circulation to her thighs, and comfortable shoes sans heels made up the majority of her daily wear now. Even though she didn't feel very bright, she chose a vibrant blue dress that she would wear over black leggings. Silver dangling earrings and a sapphire necklace completed the outfit.

Yes. It would work. She summoned a smile and looked herself over in the mirror. This would fool all of them; except perhaps Elric. While she missed the rapport her magic had allowed them to share, she was also grateful that the wolf could not get into her mind. At least not until she had a chance to do some major housekeeping in there.

She was convinced that if she faked something long enough, it would become truth.

Before she could second-guess anything, the doorbell rang. Walking through the house, she could make out voices and knew that it was Fionna and Glen. They were always early because Fionna was terrified of ever showing up late to an event and making a bad impression on someone.

"Hello, ladies," Torie said with a smile as she swung open the door.

"Hello yourself," said Fionna. She held up a bottle of wine, offering it to Torie.

"Fionna, I told you not to worry about bringing anything."

"We aren't up north," said Fionna. "No way we're showing up empty-handed."

Torie took the wine and stepped aside, letting her guests file in. Glen gave her a quick peck on the cheek and a squeeze on her upper arm as she passed.

"So, are you okay?" asked Fionna, spinning to face her friend.

"Yeah, I am. It's a beautiful day out. I'm glad the weather is finally turning."

"Oh not that," said Fionna. "I mean how are you doing with the loss of your magic?" Glen gave her a light elbow and a knowing look. "What? We're here to support her. But no one cares about the weather."

Torie chuckled good-heartedly. "Well, I care about the weather. But as for the other thing...I'm doing okay. I'm adjusting."

"I'm sorry," said Glen. "We certainly don't need to talk about this." She gave her wife another side eye glance.

"It's okay," said Torie. "I'm just trying to decide what to call myself. I'm not a witch anymore; but not sure I feel like a normal human either." She shrugged as she ushered them into the kitchen. "I didn't have a lot of time today to get much together, but please help yourself."

She took the bottle of wine Fionna had given her and added it to the collection on the island.

"There's already a bottle open, so feel free to help your-self," she said.

"Where's Jasmin?" asked Fionna. "I was sure she'd be here already."

"She texted. She's on her way."

"Any word from her sister?" Fionna asked.

Torie shook her head. She didn't want to think about the possibility that Jasmin's sister could help her regain her powers. The chance of failure would be too devastating.

"So are the guys coming over tonight?" Fionna asked.

"Not tonight," said Torie. "I thought it might be good to just have a girls' night for once." She noticed the look Glen gave her but refused to meet her eyes.

"Fine by me," added Fionna. "One on one they are fine. But the two of them together have a lot of testosterone."

Glen laughed. "That's because you haven't spent a lot

of time around men. It's just how they interact when they are together."

Fionna frowned. "Whatever. But honestly, the whole who is the- more- butch gets old fast."

Glen walked over to the island and started munching on some cheese. "So, have you seen much of Elric lately?" she asked, not looking up.

Torie started to answer, but a knock at the door interrupted her.

"And that would be Jasmin," she said, thankful for the distraction.

She opened the door, happy to see her friend and mentor. Just like Fionna, Jasmin came bearing a casserole dish and a paper bag.

"I brought some chicken buffalo dip and toasted pita chips," she said, leaning in to kiss Torie on the cheek. "I made it extra fattening…cos why the hell not."

"You didn't have to," said Torie, even though the smell of the dish made her stomach rumble.

"Oh I know. I wanted to." She breezed in, blowing past Torie with a smile. Walking into the kitchen, she exchanged greetings with Glen and Fionna and plopped her dish onto the island. "Oh good, plenty of wine. You know us so well."

"I have an idea," said Torie. "Why don't we sit out on the patio? It's a gorgeous day, and I could do with a little air."

They gathered the platters and headed out to the patio that overlooked a serene backyard that led to a line of old growth trees. Fionna made a second trip inside to get the glasses and wine before everyone settled on the teak furniture admiring the beauty of the fall colors that were just beginning to settle over the forestry.

"I love it back here," said Torie. Her voice was low and

her eyes took in the scenery without seeming to focus on any one aspect.

"How does it feel?" asked Jasmin.

Torie knew what she meant. Being able to sense her surroundings on a deeper level than just her normal five senses was something she had not even realized she possessed until it was gone.

"It's different. I'm not going to lie. Actually, it's almost scary at night."

"How's so?" asked Fionna.

"I can't explain it. I come out here and I feel like there are eyes on me. I never felt like that before."

"You're going to have to readjust to how you perceive nature," said Jasmin. "Your human senses are very different from the way your magic let you experience the world around you."

"Well, maybe she doesn't have to get accustomed to that,' added Fionna. "Has your sister gotten back to you yet?"

Jasmin didn't say anything, just looked sadly at the glass of wine she held.

"I'm sorry, Torie. Nothing yet. But she's always been a little flaky. Dropping out of touch and then springing back up unexpectedly. She'll get back to me. I'm sure of it."

Torie offered a smile. "It's really okay, Jasmin. I mean, I knew what I was doing. I still say it was worth it."

Even Fionna didn't argue that point. Torie's selfless act had probably saved them all.

"You know, even if my sister doesn't get back to me, I haven't given up. I'm still researching everything I can find about restoring a witch's powers. Plus, I'm calling in some favors with other witches in the area. Together, we'll find something."

Torie smiled and reached out, giving her friend's arm a light squeeze. "Thank you, Jasmin, I know you're doing everything you can. So no more talk about lost magic, okay?" said Torie. "I want to know what's going on with you guys?" She arched an eyebrow at them when no one spoke. "Well don't everyone talk at once."

"Well, we have news," said Glen, glancing over at Fionna. "I'm taking a new job."

"Oh yeah, doing what?" asked Jasmin.

"I'm starting a private first-responder business. One that focuses on the supernatural community. I spent so much time patching you guys up that I realized there was a market for it in town. I've been working with Max to potentially team up with the police division to deal with calls that most humans wouldn't understand."

"Wow," said Torie. "That's a great idea."

"Well, I figured that as long as you three are together, I probably won't have any shortage of business. Plus, at least this way I'll feel like I'm more of a help to you. Not just another non-supernatural who gets in the way."

She caught herself and gave a Torie a sharp, pained look.

"I am so sorry. I didn't mean that the way it sounded."

The fact that she made her friends uncomfortable made Torie feel awful.

"No, I didn't take it any way that wasn't intended. Besides, you have never not been helpful to us. I've always been thankful you were around with your trusty bag of medicines."

"It's been really well received," said Fionna. "We spent yesterday dropping her card off at some of the supernatural congregating spots around town. Just kind of getting the word out."

Just then, Glen's phone chirped, making everyone jump. She pulled it out of her pocket, frowning at the number that came up. Swiping at the screen, she held it to her ear.

"Hello?" She paused, nodding to herself. "I'll be right there." She slid it back into her pocket and looked at the others, excitement spreading over her face.

"Who was that?" asked Fionna.

"Talk about timing," Glen replied. "That was the owner of Jim's Bakery. He said a fight just broke out and there are a couple of supernaturals with injuries that need attention."

"A fight?" said Jasmin. "At...the coffee shop? This I gotta see."

Torie was on her feet and heading back into the house. She grabbed her keys from the console and headed for the door. "Well, what are we waiting for? I'll drive."

How Torie Got Her Hex Back:
Chapter Two

They pulled up to the bakery in Torie's old Subaru and saw about a half-dozen people milling about on the sidewalk outside the shop. Before they could get out of the car, Jim, the owner, was racing towards them.

"Thank goodness you're here," he said to Glen. "I didn't know who to call. I mean, I love Sheriff Max and all, but I don't want my patrons being carted off to jail, and I sure don't want any unnecessary eyes prying into my business."

"What happened?" asked Jasmin.

He motioned for them to follow him. "Come on in and see for yourself."

They made their way into the bakery that Torie had come to think of as her home away from home. She had spent many mornings there, sitting in the comfortable leather chairs opposite the large, stone fireplace chatting away with Fionna and Jasmin. But for the first time since she had moved to Singing Falls, she felt ill at ease walking into the space.

Something was clawing at the back of her mind; and it made her skin crawl.

The place was in shambles. Coffee tables were upended, chairs had been tossed haphazardly about. The display counter that contained assorted homemade sweets and breads had been shattered, and one of the girls that worked behind the counter was sitting on the floor, back propped against the wall with a towel stained with blood held against her head.

Glen moved over to her first, bending down next to her and starting her examination.

"Jim, what happened here?" asked Jasmin, trying to take in the scene.

"I have no idea. One minute everything was fine; typical crowd. The next, chairs are flying and people were at each other's throats."

Torie looked around, taking mental snapshots of the crowd milling outside the large picture window and the ones still inside the shop. From the looks of things, it had been a busy evening. Nothing unusual about that. Torie could see where many of the patrons had been enjoying a cup of coffee with the delicious pastries the bakery was known for.

"Do you know who started it?" queried Jasmin.

Jim shrugged. "It all happened so fast. But I will say that the first blows were thrown by Jake Pressin and Mikey Belvin."

Jasmin gave him a surprised look.

"Those two are pretty much just kids. Good ones too. I can't see them throwing punches at anyone."

"You would think," said Jim. "But I'm telling you what I saw. There was nothing sweet about them. They had this crazed look in their eyes. Like they were just focused on one thing; hurting the other."

Jasmin wandered over to where Torie was looking around.

"Maybe those two were fighting over a girl. One of them said something to the other that was unflattering and...bam. Fight."

Jasmin shook her head. "Not those two. Jake is a rabbit shifter and Mikey is an empath. It isn't in either of their natures to come to physical blows. It's just not who they are."

Torie looked around, surveying the damage.

"Hey, Jim," she called, "was it just the two of them that did all this?"

"No," he replied. "It was like a scene out of a television show; once they threw the first punches, everyone in the place jumped up and started fighting. It was crazy."

Torie moved to the side of the room opposite the large fireplace. There was a small table for two that had not been disturbed. The white tablecloth was unruffled. There were two small plates, each with a slice of half-eaten carrot cake, and two cups of what appeared to be cinnamon tea. Torie looked at the setting and then glanced at the chaos around it.

Why hadn't it been overtaken by the wave of violence that washed over everything else?

"Jim, who was sitting here?" she asked.

The owner looked at the table and shook his head. "Sorry, I don't remember."

Torie started to tell him that was okay, but her attention was quickly drawn to a couple who had been peering into the wrecked place through the doorway. One yelled at the other and asked him to step back. The second man apparently took great affront to being spoken to that way and yelled back in response.

"Hey now," said Jim, stepping between them. "What's going on here?"

"He said your oatmeal cookies taste like they have almonds in them, and I said they taste more like walnuts," yelled one of the men. "He obviously doesn't know what he's talking about."

"You're a fool," said the second man, his voice rising. "You obviously wouldn't know a walnut if it walked up and punched you."

The first man bristled. "Oh yeah? How's this walnut taste?" He reached past Jim to swing at the man, his fist just grazing the man's jaw.

A roar escaped the one who was hit, and before anyone could step in, he shifted into a large bear, tossing Jim aside like a rag doll. The second man huffed audibly in and out of his nose. His breath sounded like the bellows of a forge, feeding a fire with its mighty wind. He shifted into a large bull, wide and muscular, the span of his horns nearly touching both walls either side of him. Someone outside screamed as patrons ran for cover.

The two shifters stared at one another, eyes glowing with hatred.

"Okay, that's enough!" screamed Jasmin.

She stepped forward, her hands clasped in front of her. Then she quickly separated them, sending an explosive shockwave outward that knocked the two shifters away from one another.

Their massive bodies crashed into walls and stonework, shaking the shop. Each of them struggled to their feet but immediately shifted back to human form. They were groggy, unsteady on their feet, holding their heads in their hands.

"What...what happened?" asked one of the men, looking around.

"You just tried to gore your friend here," said Jasmin, pointing at the bear shifter who was still trying to make his way to his feet.

"What? No. I...I would never do that."

Jasmin and Torie exchanged looks. Something was definitely amiss here.

"See that little lady over there with the black medicine bag?" said Jasmin. "Why don't you both go over there and let her look at you. We'll talk about what just happened later."

Torie rushed over to Jim's side. Fionna was there, trying to help the man to his feet.

"Did you see that?" Jim said, wincing at the pain that was rifling through his body. "Just like before. I've seen those two in here together many times. They're friends. But I'd swear if it weren't for Jasmin, one of them would have killed the other."

"He's right," said Fionna. "I could feel their anger. It was white hot. And there was something else as well..." her voice trailed off as a frown creased her brow.

"Fi, can you give me a hand here?" called Glen from behind the counter. She was starting to treat more of the cafe patrons who appeared to have suffered minor cuts and bruises.

"Coming!" said Fionna, bouncing for the back of the room.

"Well?" said Torie, as Jasmin walked back to her. "What did you feel?"

Jasmin shook her head. "I didn't feel anything. Just two men about to come to blows over cookies. It makes no sense whatsoever."

"You've been around supernaturals a lot longer than me," said Torie. "Could this just be part of their normal behavior? Something you're just now witnessing?"

"I don't think so. I mean, they were genuinely confused as to what was going on when they shifted back to human form. Like they didn't remember what set them off."

Torie found herself cursing her lack of magic. Again.

Just then, the sound of heavy boots crunching broken glass beneath them interrupted their conversation. They turned just as Sheriff Max walked up to them.

"Jasmin, Torie," he said, nodding at them in greeting.

"I thought Jim wasn't calling you?" Torie said.

"He didn't. Someone called into 9-1-1 to say that some of the special townfolk were having a quarrel at the coffee shop. Thought I'd see what it was about."

He whistled as he looked around, taking in the scene.

"Care to let me in on what happened?" he asked.

"Would if I could, Sheriff," said Jasmin. "But, honestly, we have no idea. People just seemed to flip and go at each other for a minute. But things seemed to have calmed down now."

The big sheriff nodded and then cocked his head to the side and sniffed the air, closing his eyes.

"What is it?" asked Torie. "You pick something up?"

"Magic," he said. "Just a whiff…now it's gone." Wolves were notorious for their sense of smell.

"That would be me," said Jasmin. "I had to whip up a little force field to separate two of the combatants."

Max nodded. "That would explain it then."

Torie snapped her finger. "Max, I have an idea. Would you come with me?"

The wolf frowned. "What are you doing involved in this Torie? You don't have any powers anymore."

She started, annoyed at his bluntness. "I know that. But it doesn't mean I can't hang out with my friends while they do...witchy things. Anyway, just follow me."

She led him to the back wall where the one table that had not been disturbed sat.

"Can you tell who was sitting here?" she asked.

Max looked around, to make sure no one was looking, and then leaned down to sniff the table. His face shimmered, shifting slightly; just enough to let his snout lengthen and thicken as his jawline receded into more lupine features. He took a deep breath through his nostrils, moving his face from side to side across the tabletop. Then he stood up, his face back to its normal handsome features.

"One person, female, human. Sat right there," he pointed to the left side of the table.

"And the other person?" asked Torie.

He shook his head. "There wasn't anyone else."

Torie looked from one side of the table to the other, pointing at the two distinct sets of dishes.

"You can see that there are clearly two partially eaten pieces of cake sitting on two different plates. Two different cups of tea and two different sets of silverware. She wasn't alone."

"I can see that, but I'm telling you what my nose told me. There was only one person sitting here. This side—" he gestured to the right side of the table, "—was vacant. No smell or trace of anyone or anything."

"That doesn't seem right."

He shrugged. "All I know is that I trust my nose; even more so than my eyes. And my nose says there was no one here."

He excused himself and went back to speak with Jim, eager to take the owner's statement.

Torie frowned and stood with her arms crossed, surveying the table. Then, glancing around to see if anyone was watching, she closed her eyes and held one hand over the table. She stood like that for nearly a full minute before being interrupted by someone clearing their throat. She spun around to see Jasmin staring intently at her.

"Anything?" Jasmin asked.

Torie let out a deep breath. "No. Of course not. I don't know what I keep hoping for."

Jasmin smiled warmly. "Keep hope alive, my friend. I still have some ideas to help with this."

Torie returned her smile but said nothing. She wasn't quite ready to give up on thinking that maybe one day her magic would return, but she also wasn't in the mood to get her hopes up only to have them dashed.

"What did Max say? Does he know who was sitting here?"

Torie shook her head. "He said there was only one person sitting here, A human woman. But no one else."

"Huh," said Jasmin. "That's weird."

"So now what?" said Torie. "Seems like there isn't anything more to this than random violence."

"Violence is never random. There is always a reason. We just need to figure out what it was."

They made their way back to the front of the building and walked outside.

"I guess we could talk to the people still hanging around," said Torie. "See if they saw anything that could explain what happened."

Jasmin agreed, and soon they had spoken to almost everyone outside the cafe. When they finished, Fionna and Glen came out to join them.

"How is everyone?" asked Torie.

"Bruised," said Glen. "A few cuts here and there, but for the most part, it was all superficial."

"Do any of them remember what started the melee?" asked Jasmin.

"No one knows anything. The two that Jasmin separated didn't even remember shifting," she added.

"Well, I think we've done all we can here. Looks like we won't be having our usual coffee and scones here tomorrow," said Torie. "This place is a mess."

"I'll swing by your place in the morning," said Jasmin. "Like I said, there is something I want to try. You make the coffee; I'll bring the treats."

They headed out, past the thinning crowd that was quickly losing interest in the goings-on at one of the local supernatural gathering spots in town.

They didn't notice the tall, pretty woman with afro-puffs that had been watching them intently through rose-colored sunglasses. Once they were in their cars and had left the drive, the young woman slipped around the back of the building where a window provided an unobstructed view of Max speaking with the shop owner.

She smiled. This was going to be easier than expected.

Grab your copy...
vinci-books.com/toriehex

About the Author

M.J. Caan is an avid reader and writer of all things science fiction and fantasy. Author of multiple science fiction and paranormal fantasy series, M.J. likes to think that there is still magic out there in the world. Even if it's only between the pages of a great book.